MASTERSON

MASTERSON SERIES BOOK ONE

LISA LANG BLAKENEY

WRITERGIRL PRESS

LICENSE NOTE

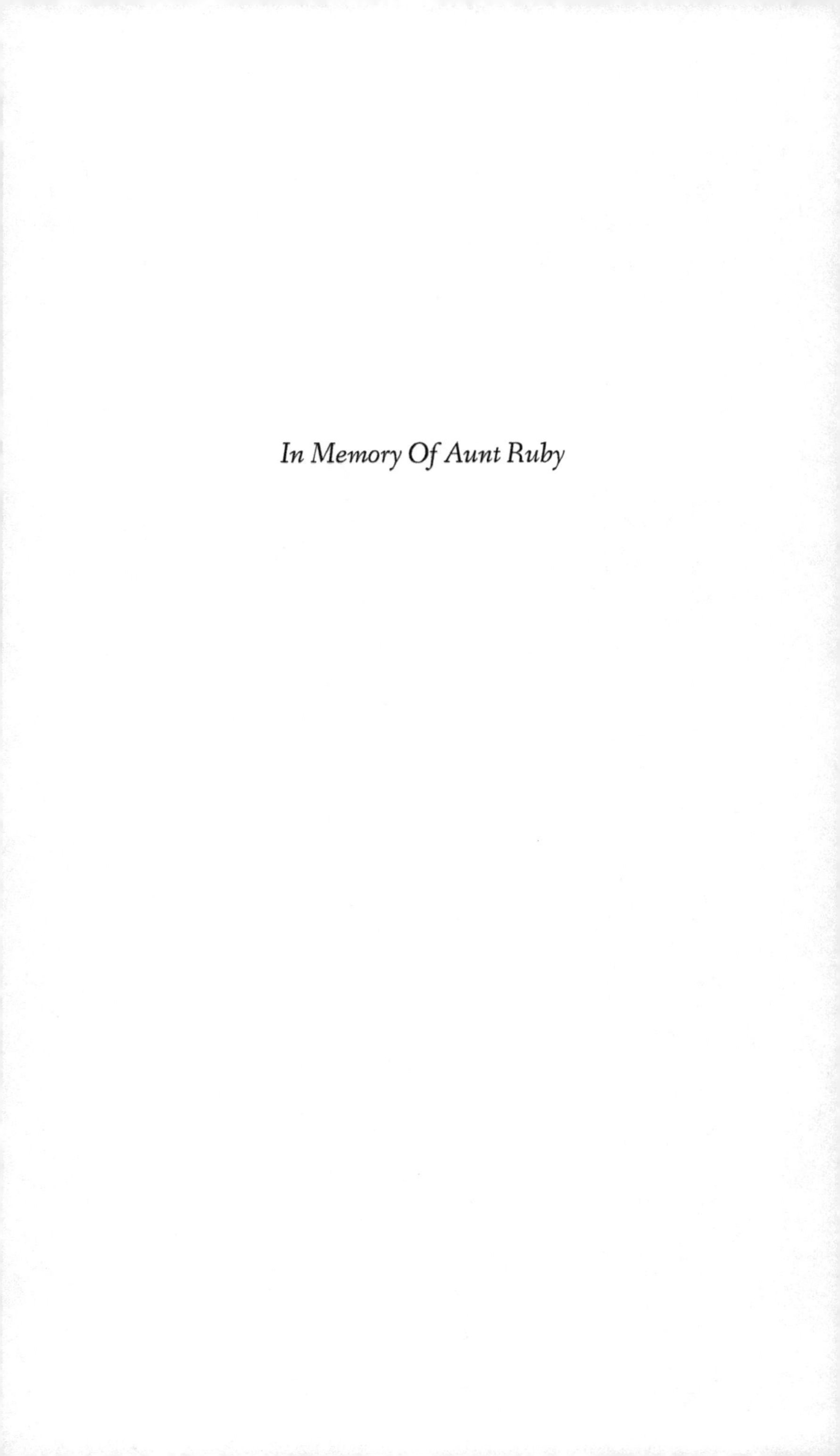

In Memory Of Aunt Ruby

PRAISE FOR MASTERSON

"Intense. Explosive. Panty Melting. Raw. Exposed. Angst. Multifaceted."

- Snuggled Up With My BFF

"Cover to cover, page by page every word was amazing. This author is amazing and her work is even more amazing. She really can get all the details and words to sound great together.Yes I want more and crave more I just couldn't get enough of Roman and Elizabeth. "

- Whispered Thoughts Book Blog

"As soon as I picked up book 1 I was addicted to this series. I couldn't wait for this one to come out! I absolutely love Roman and Elizabeth together!"

- Badass Betties Book Blog

"I definitely recommend this series to readers. It was the first of its kind that I have read, and I was not disappointed. 5 Stars!"

- Booksessions

BOOKS BY LISA

The Masterson Series

Devour this addictive series about the possessive bad boy, Roman Masterson, who falls hard and fast for the girl he's promised his family to protect.

Masterson

Masterson Unleashed

Masterson In Love

Masterson Made

Joseph Loves Juliette

Masterson Box Set

Masterson Next Generation Series

The crazy hot fruit doesn't fall far from the tree. Dive into this second generation of Masterson men!

Knox - Knox & Gigi

Bronx - Bronx & Karma

Seven - Coming soon!

The King Brothers Series

Dive into this series of interconnected standalones featuring 3 alpha hot brothers and the women they lay claim to without apology.

Claimed - Camden & Jade

Indebted - Cutter & Sloan

Broken - Stone & Tiny

Promised - All King Brothers

King Brothers Box Set

The Nighthawk Series

Sexy & sweet sports romances set in the professional world of football. All standalones.

Saint - Saint & Sabrina

Wolf - Cooper & Ursula

Diesel - Mason & Olivia

Jett - Jett & Adrienne

Rush - Rush & Mia

Freak - Freak & Willow

Brick - coming soon!

CLAIMED

Meet Alpha Camden King
Free For A Limited Time!
Available FREE through this link only.

"I tracked you, I found you, and I'm not leaving until I get what I came for."

DOWNLOAD NOW
Also available in Audio + Paperback.

She's a sweet girl in trouble. He's a bad boy asked to protect her. Their chemistry is undeniable but it's an attraction that's completely off-limits to explore. That was their first mistake...

After Elizabeth Hill is brutally attacked in her apartment by an intruder and then unceremoniously dumped by her ex-boyfriend, she moves in with family that she barely knows for protection. All she remembers about Roman is that he was the moody, mean boy who played a cruel trick on her when she was just six years old; but soon learns that he is now a complex and multi-layered man who has the ability to protect her, ignite her, and challenge her like no one ever has before.

Wealthy Roman Masterson makes his fortune by fixing celebrity problems for big money and by any means necessary. He is a foul-mouthed, bad-tempered, playboy who doesn't have the time or inclination to babysit a gullible little brat from the suburbs...until he unknowingly spots her in the middle of a crowded dance floor and decides right then and there that she belongs with him. Little does he know that the woman he craves is the same girl he's been sworn to protect.

Author Note: Please note that this installment of the series ends on a cliffhanger.

ONE

ELIZABETH

I NOTICE THAT ETHAN HAS an unusually glazed look in his eyes when he pops his head up from under my tangerine strapless sundress, which he has leisurely pushed up right above my hips. He has been licking and lapping between my legs for several minutes in a grand effort to get me primed for what is to come next, and he looks like he is definitely ready to give it to me as soon as I give him the go ahead.

"You like that, Bitsy?"

His mouth turns into a goofy grin. One that I've always been unable to resist. Although I thought I had made it perfectly clear that I hadn't waited all this time to have sex with Ethan just to give it up casually, unplanned, or on a whim. Yet somehow I find myself spread eagle, on top of my brand new tufted pink comforter, panties God knows where, and nervous as all hell.

I know full well that having sex will change everything between us, which is why I've been especially careful about the when and the where ... up until now. We weren't even supposed to be here tonight, but Ethan's car was acting funny; so it was either chill at my place or end the night early.

"Don't pull your top off yet," he whispers in my ear as an attempt to sound seductive. Unfortunately, Ethan's attempt at being sexy comes off somewhat awkward, and his request for me to keep my top on seems just... wrong.

"Why?" I ask while lowering my arms from above my head. "You haven't even touched my boobs yet."

"Don't need to touch 'em right now. Relax and just trust me."

Don't need to touch them? What the heck was he talking about? Ethan had been rubbing, kneading and sucking on my breasts since we started going out, getting me ready for what I guess was this very moment.

Usually when we played around in his dad's old Audi after one of our dates, he couldn't keep his hands off of the girls, and I loved it. I thought he did too. I know he chugged down a beer or two when we were watching television earlier, but something seems off with him. I'm just not sure what it is. Yet when he says those last three words, "just trust me" and flashes me a smile with his lips still moist from earnestly eating me out, my decision is already made.

As far as boyfriends go, I know that I've hit the jackpot, at least among my small inner circle of friends. I've known Ethan since my freshman year of U Penn, and girls have always fallen all over themselves when they're around him. Not much has changed since graduation; they still do.

When our friendship started to evolve into more during our senior year, I made the decision to take things super slow, because I am quite aware of Ethan's sexual history. Not wanting to be just another one of his conquests, I've been making him wait for over a year to have sex with me, and he's been quite patient, but I'm not sure how much longer he's going to wait for me.

Truth be told, I'm not sure how much longer I can even wait. I mean, I'm not a virgin. I'm just very selective about who I give it to, especially since I seemed to have picked so badly in the past. My high school boyfriend was a Grade A jerk.

"Okay," I murmur softly. "I trust you."

Wait. Over.

I lower my lids in an effort to do as he asks and simply relax and enjoy the moment, but Ethan's cell phone starts ringing for what is the third time in the last 15 minutes. He stops touching me and reaches over the side of the bed to check the screen. Immediately I imagine the worst, and I think he notices the distrust written all over my face.

While Ethan has been a pretty good boyfriend to me, being with him has made me the target of dirty looks from girls we went to school with and beyond. He's definitely good looking, but he's also a very promising swimmer who is training for the next Summer Olympics. Many girls see fame and endorsement dollars when they look at him, and I know that many have the capability of being downright ruthless in order to get who and what they want. So I keep my eyes and ears open. Constantly. It's exhausting sometimes, but my mother once told me that every man has their Achilles' heel, and my fear is that the vagina is Ethan's.

"It's just Thomas. I'm going to turn it off," he tries to assure me in an effort to keep me present in the moment.

"That was Thomas who called you all three times?" I ask knowing good and well it was probably that slutty girl Penny from my old Econ class calling him. A total sorority slut, she was notorious for throwing what was between her legs at every halfway decent looking boy on campus, and I'd heard that she was just as busy with the graduates. Especially jocks like Ethan.

"Yeah, but he doesn't want anything. I'll call him later. We're busy, right babe?"

I assume that question is Ethan's not-so-subtle way of checking to make sure I'm still on board, so I nod my head in agreement. He smiles and continues his seduction by slowly gliding the palms of his smooth hands up my thighs while pushing my dress up even further under my breasts to deliver a few feathery kisses around my navel.

Just when I think he is going to actually take my dress completely off and continue with his leisurely stroll around my body, he skips ahead and makes his way to my lips, shoving his tongue inside, rapidly moving it back and forth in my mouth.

Kissing Ethan is typically a nice experience, but like I said, something is off. His kisses seem sloppy and amateurish, and as he is getting more excited, I am starting to feel smothered under the weight of his large body and the faint smell and taste of beer on his breath.

"You ready for me, Bitsy?" He asks using my nickname in his deepest baritone voice.

Reluctantly I shake my head yes, although all the flashing signs in my head are telling me to STOP! I don't want this to be my first time with him. Not here, not like this. But then I consider what would happen if I attempted to stop him. Would he be angry with me? Would he want to end things? Would he tell his friends that I'm frigid? Would he start taking Penny's calls? Wouldn't it just be better to get it over with? Rip the band-aid off, so to speak.

Trust me, I am seriously considering slapping my own self for having these sorts of insecure thoughts, but I have little control over what pathetic things pop into my head at any given time. I know that these are totally the wrong reasons to have sex with someone, but is there ever truly a perfect moment? There hasn't been one yet. Maybe I'm overthinking this whole thing.

Ethan stops and looks wildly in my eyes for a moment. I've never seen this look before. It's as if he needs me in a way that he never has. I've been pretty quiet this whole time, and God knows he's waited a long time for this to happen. So I decide to go ahead and give him the assurance he needs.

I touch the right side of his face gently with my palm. "Go ahead, Ethan."

His face relaxes since that seems to be just what he needs to hear. He reaches in his back pocket and pulls out a condom, opens the foil packet, and rolls it onto his long but rather slender penis. I do my best not to ruin the mood by asking him why he even has a condom so conveniently on his person. I can't imagine that he thought that this was going to definitely happen, but I don't want to sound like the insecure girlfriend.

I worry for a split second about pregnancy because the condom seems really thin, like it could easily snap like an old rubber band pulled too tautly. But maybe that's how all condoms look. I never really watched the only other guy I've had sex with put his condoms on. I was in high school and too embarrassed to really look. Obviously I had no business having sex with him either.

Ethan lowers himself back down and gently starts kissing the side of my neck. It feels relaxing, but as he starts to slowly poke and prod his way into my opening, the muscles in my neck and shoulders begin to tense up. I'm not sure why this hurts so much, like I said I've done this before, but I am seriously thinking about pushing him off and running the hell out of my own bedroom. I feel like a virgin all over again. Yet as soon as I go to open my mouth to say the word wait, he kisses me deeply and mutters in my mouth, "Hold on tight, Bitsy." So I do.

As he pushes further inside me with several hard thrusts, I flinch from the unfamiliar fullness, but he doesn't notice my discomfort because his head is burrowed so far into the side of my neck now. He groans while methodically pumping and pushing inside me for a few more minutes, then he speeds up for a few seconds, right before he completely collapses on top of me. He's so frackin' heavy.

"Oh shit!" he cries out. "Bitsy, you're amaz—"

Before I can even process whatever that anticlimactic moment was that just passed between us, we both jump at an unexpectedly loud crash. It sounds like someone has just rammed their head completely through one of my front windows.

Ethan jerks his head up, leans his torso over the side of the bed, and reaches underneath for his phone.

"Fuck!" He starts furiously texting someone.

I'm frozen in place as quick, thunderous footsteps are moving towards our direction while Ethan quickly pulls up his sweatpants and fixes my dress. They're moving so quickly down the hall, I know it's just a matter of seconds before they reach us.

"Hide in the closet!" Ethan frantically orders.

My heart pounds with brute force from fear.

They're inside the room before I have a chance to move.

A man in an all black sweatsuit and wearing a Shrek Halloween face mask (of all cliché things) bellows the words, "Don't fucking move."

I freeze in place and so does Ethan. There are two other men, also dressed in all black with black knit ski masks standing next to the one doing all the talking. They are silent, but the two of them are holding sleek metal gray handguns aimed at Ethan's head.

"Sit," Shrek orders.

I'm not sure who he's talking to, but I immediately sit straight down on the edge of my bed with my mouth closed and my legs shut. I smell like latex and sex, and my body trembles with fear when I take a brief glance up at the intruder's face. Even behind his mask, I can tell that Shrek is dead in the eyes. His cold glare makes the hairs on the back of my neck stand up and shiver.

"Where is my shit?" Shrek asks Ethan.

"I don't know what you're talking about," he replies without enough fear in his voice in my opinion. Does he know who they are? Why isn't he scared?

"I don't know what you're talking about," Shrek parrots back in a sing-song voice. "Oh yes, the fuck you do know what I'm talking about. You're high on my shit right fucking now, and if you don't give me ALL my product and I do mean all of it in the next five minutes, I'm going to have to hurt your very pretty girlfriend over here. And I promise you that she won't be pretty no more after I'm done. Then you're next."

I'm silently crying at this point and paralyzed with fear. I strangely consider all the crime and cop shows that I have mindlessly watched all my life and wonder what the victims would do in this situation. I've always thought that if I were to ever find myself in a compromised situation, that I would be smart enough to save myself. Yet now that the time is upon me, I'm not sure what the hell to do.

Should I make a run for it? Should I beg for our lives? Where's my cell phone? Hell, I'm really frightened, and I have no idea how to get us out of this. I'm just seriously praying that Ethan will give these guys whatever the hell it is they want, so they'll leave. I'm very much invested in living another day with my face intact.

Ethan puffs his chest out. "Like I said, man, I don't know what you're talking about."

Shrek grins sinisterly.

"That was the wrong answer, Aqua Man."

And that's when a black leather covered fist cracks me square in the jaw.

Then everything fades to black.

TWO

ELIZABETH

THREE WEEKS LATER

VIBRATIONS OF BASS HEAVY techno music pulse throughout my sweat covered body as I twirl and gyrate my body in the middle of the dance floor. I'm a pro at this, so I'm careful not to spill a drop of the merlot that swishes around in my wine glass as I get my groove on. I just hold the glass high and close to my ear while my hips and feet do all the work of keeping to the monotonous but primal beat that is driving all the demons right out of my soul. It's been three weeks, give or take a day, since I woke up with the worst headache of my life and my life in shambles. For just one night, though, I don't want to think about any of that. For just one night, I want to dance.

I'm starting to think the deejay is my soul mate or a simply brilliant human being, because when my favorite part of the song comes on he performs a variety of scratches on his computerized turntables to extend that portion of the song, and I frackin' love him for it. I throw back my wine glass and take a long final sip, placing the empty glass on the nearest littered high-top table; and then I begin to truly offer myself like a Santeria sacrifice over to the music. All I need is a long white flowing dress and a live chicken.

Unlike some of my body thrashing counterparts who basically lose their minds when the computerized beat comes on, I close my eyes, raise my arms high above my head, and slowly sway my very pear shaped hips to the bottom of the song. The bass. As I do, I can feel the vino traveling intravenously through my veins relieving me of all my anxiety and insecurities. It feels good. No, it feels great.

Unfortunately, my euphoria comes to a screeching halt, when I start to feel the large body of an intoxicated stranger slowly dancing up behind me. Initially my body tightens in fear, but because I don't want to overreact in public, I decide not to respond immediately to his presence. Not every stranger is out to hurt me. I need to remember that if I'm going to live in the world.

I consider the fact that in a club where most dancers are moving at the speed of a Zumba class, my dancing can appear more slow and sexual than the average person's, and that's why I make the decision to cut the drunk guy some slack. Plus, this is the best part of the song. I want to finish enjoying it. Unfortunately, the dickwad takes this as some sort of approval to move things a step further, and that's when I feel the drunken stranger up on my ass. I know his hands are probably going to be next.

Sure enough, I feel a hand firmly start to grip the left side of my hips, and can feel one of his sweaty fingers touching the exposed skin above my waistline (thanks to the halter top I'm wearing). So I stop dancing, turn around, and see the red-nosed face of a kid who probably isn't even twenty-one yet and hasn't quite learned when he's reached his limit.

I use my pointer finger to call him over even closer so he

can hear me. He doesn't seem to understand that I'm annoyed, because he has a wide grin plastered across his face, when it's blatantly obvious that I don't.

"Are you drunk?" I ask him like I'm his older sister.

"Not yet, gorgeous," he says in a drunk, flirty voice.

"Well, listen up, junior, this is a solo gig," I tell him in his ear. "I don't need a partner."

The look on the kid's face is priceless. He's embarrassed, and I think he starts to look around to make sure that no one heard what I just said to him. As if someone could actually hear me over the high decibel level of the music or even see us in this dim lighting. He's not a jerk about what I just said to him, though. He gives me a slight head nod, turns, and walks off the dance floor. Confrontation averted.

It's at that exact moment that I consider just for a moment that maybe the kid had it right. Maybe someone was watching us, because I swear that I can feel the stare of a faceless shadow in a far corner of the club. To the left of the main bar.

You would think that I wouldn't notice a shadow based on the many moving bodies around me, but that's the thing; people are dancing, laughing, talking, ordering drinks, walking around. Even people at the bar are fidgeting, adjusting their seats, talking to whoever is next to them or trying to grab the bartender's attention. Everyone in the whole place is moving. Everyone but that one solitary, faceless shape in the corner.

A chill runs down my spine and I turn away. I'm a little freaked out, but I know that I need to shake it off. Ever since the attack, I've been jumpy and on edge. What I need is another drink. That will calm me down.

Now that I am entirely out of my zone and know that the deejay will be changing the song soon, I decide to head back over to the bar and straight towards the handsome bartender in the white tee. I spotted him earlier and liked the looks of him. He looks safe.

I grab the last remaining stool and scan the crowd for my partner in crime, Sloan. I have no idea where she has wandered off to and while we're both grown; I think it was breaking the girl code for her to just leave me to fend for myself inside a club. Especially after everything that I've been through over the last few weeks. I take another quick glance to look for the creep in the corner, but notice that whoever or whatever it was is no longer there. I'm relieved.

"He took you out of your groove, huh?"

I raise a curious eyebrow, because I mistakenly think the bartender is talking about the shadow in the corner, but soon realize that he's referring to the beer boy from the dance floor.

"Here you go. Another glass of red on the house. I don't know where these club virgins are coming from all of a sudden. They're ruining the vibe in here. The doorman isn't doing his job. That kid doesn't even look old enough to be in here."

Another glass of wine? Oh, I am definitely headed into hangover territory, but I smile, accept the drink, and start slurping it down as if it were my first of the night.

"Thank you, umm—"

"The name's Marco and you are?" He asks showcasing a set of pearly white teeth while wiping down the bar top. Was he flirting? Hell, I don't know and I don't want to know. I'm sure he's just being friendly like most bartenders.

Men are completely off the menu for me now.

"Elizabeth."

"You're not here alone, are you?"

"No, I came with a friend."

Some friend. Where the hell is she?

During the cab ride here, my best friend Sloan bragged for twenty minutes that she was bringing me to the uber-exclusive Club Lotus. Per her words, it was, "beyond the red velvet rope." There was no rope. In fact, there was only an inconspicuous looking gray metal door that you knocked on, which was then answered by a very unhappy-looking man who asked very gruffly for your ID. Three minutes later the man either let you in the door or he told you to scram.

Sloan's ID must have checked out, so they permitted us inside once he jotted down my driver's license information inside a red, leather covered journal. Another thing that gives me the jitters, but which Sloan assures me is totally safe. Once past the forgettable gray door, I couldn't believe the unforgettable and intoxicating world that we stepped into.

Club Lotus is a beautifully designed dance club, housed in a hundred-year-old but expertly renovated center city bank, with broad, polished mahogany bars, massive pillars, and intricately carved high ceilings bathed in soft champagne colored chandelier lighting. It is everything that I imagined it to be. The grandness. The sexiness. The exclusivity of it. While there are definitely cozy little seating areas and an elevated VIP section, it doesn't seem like an overly pretentious club, although I know that most of the people in here probably make at least six figures or better.

I'm fascinated watching many of the high-powered corporate women enter through the metal door and walk straight back to a large locker room, where they hang their very expensive designer suits and change into their very small, body conscious dresses for the night. Most of the men look like new money as well. Powerful, but definitely not uptight.

Sloan fits right in. She's on the fast track as a pharmaceutical sales rep for one of the biggest companies in the country and makes a great living. I don't fit in as much, but I strive to one day. I can't wait to blend into the shiny and slick fabric of the city and its people, and to be able to afford to buy five-dollar lattes every day, although it feels like nothing is clicking into place for me these days.

I continue looking for Sloan as I take several more sips of wine, but she is still M.I.A. Fortunately the deejay is doing a fantastic job of keeping me distracted and begins inter-playing two songs that are calling me back to the dance floor, but I have an off feeling that I just can't shake, so I decide to stay put and flirt with the sun-kissed bartender. After about ten minutes of polite conversation between us he asks me, "So you're not going back out there gorgeous?"

I grin. "Nah, I'd rather sit here and enjoy the music."

"Hard day at work?"

"Not exactly ... more like a hard week. A bad break up."

Marco nods in understanding and then a text comes in from my mother. I don't feel like reading it, but I figure I have to because, well, it's from my mom.

Mom: Where are you?

Me: I'm out with Sloan.

Mom: That means you're dancing very inappropriately somewhere.

Me: That's very possible:)

Mom: I've come up with a solution to your situation.

Me: Really?

Mom: I called your aunt.

Me: Aunt who???

This topic really deserves a phone conversation, but there is no way I could have a meaningful conversation with my mother, half-drunk, in a noisy club. I'm surprised she's actually this good at texting. They're coming in fast and grammatically correct.

Mom: You know who I'm talking about, smarty. Aunt Juliette. The aunt I told you to give a call three weeks ago when you decided to stay in that godforsaken city after almost being murdered.

Me: When did u learn to txt like this, mom? I'm impressed.

Mom: I didn't. I speak into the phone, and it translates what I say into a text for me.

Aaah, of course.

Me: Very nice, mom.

Mom: Her number is 215-555-7890. Call her tomorrow. She has room for you until whenever.

Whenever I come to my senses and move home, she means.

Me: It won't be long. I'm figuring things out and will have a place soon.

Mom: Is business doing better?

Me: Yep.

Mom: Are you really okay, Bitsy?

Me: Yes, mom. Don't worry.

Lies.

First of all, there is no way on God's green earth that I'm going to admit to my mother that I am scared shitless after being brutally assaulted by my boyfriend's frackin' drug dealers. She doesn't even know everything that happened. She'd literally drive down to Philly, pack up my stuff, and force me to come home if she did.

When I woke up in my bedroom three weeks ago, Ethan and the assailants were gone; my head hurt like hell, and my apartment had been completely ransacked and robbed. I'd been saving tip money for over two years from my part-time job at The Tavern and storing it all in two empty tampon boxes under the bathroom sink. (I know. I'm an idiot, but I've got an issue with paying bank fees.) It was over seventeen thousand dollars, and my plan was to use that money to live on while I worked on building my business full time; but now all of that money is gone and I need a Plan B.

I was too frightened to call the police when I finally woke up, so the only person I called was Sloan, who promptly took me to the emergency room. Physically I had only suffered a minor concussion, but emotionally I was ruined.

My home had been violated, I couldn't concentrate on work, I was scared to be alone, and my boyfriend's phone was going straight to voicemail. His father, who I had only met once before, finally called me a few days later and told me that Ethan was fine and resting in a drug rehab in Arizona.

When I told him everything that transpired that night, then asked him (politely) why his son saw fit to leave me unconscious on the floor of my bedroom without even a 911 call, his father totally sidestepped my question and blatantly offered me twenty-five hundred dollars if I remained quiet about everything.

To add insult to injury, he also said there was another twenty-five hundred in it for me if I refused any and all of

Ethan's calls. Something about codependency, blah, blah, blah.

Needless to say, I turned down his highly offensive offer and told him to go fuck himself. I didn't need to be paid off to avoid having any contact with Ethan, considering that he had been ignoring all of my calls and texts for days, anyway.

Assholes.

Both of them.

And as far as my business is concerned, that is laughable at best. About eighteen months ago, I built and launched a smartphone application that helps connect college students with scholarship money.

I named the application School Bucks, and I charge ninety-nine cents per download for it. The app generates about three hundred dollars a month which is a pretty decent start, but it doesn't pay the bills. I need to make some major improvements to the app and develop a marketing plan to make some traction in the marketplace, but now that my entire savings is completely gone, I'm going to have to come up with a Plan B.

All of this on my brain is what has brought me here tonight. I'm trying to forget about how I can't get a decent night's sleep in my own home, because I'm too afraid to close my eyes. I am also trying to forget how any bit of money I earn now has to go to bills, not savings, and that I don't have enough money to put down a security deposit and first month's rent on a new place.

So I guess living at my aunt's house would be a great way to feel safe for a moment and stack some money while I figure things out. Work on my Plan B. Maybe I do need to bite the bullet and accept some help, regardless of the source. It's not like I have a lot have options. It's either this or go home to my parents and start all over again.

Oh, hell no.

Me: What would she charge me to stay there?

Mom: Nothing, you're family.

I'm not exactly comfortable with that. I'm not a deadbeat.

Me: I'll call her to discuss it. I gotta go.

Mom: Call me after you two speak.

Me: I will. Bye, mom:)

I finally have a pleasant buzz and am totally fine bobbing my head seated right where I am. I don't mind hanging around and flirting with Marco either. It's easy. While I am not quite sure if he likes men, women or both, I definitely enjoy his company as he talks about his childhood in Miami, his dream of visiting family he's never met in Cuba, and why he moved to Philadelphia. He is totally taking my mind off the fact that I may move in with a family that I haven't seen since I was a kid.

"Damn." Worry lines crinkle Marco's forehead.

"What?" I ask.

"Those two over there." He points. "See the one blond in the dress. They're arguing. When those two argue, the shit always ends badly."

"Who are they?"

"They usually come on Sunday nights. That's a whole different crowd. Younger. More hip-hop and radio. Not as exclusive of a crowd. They must not have realized that tonight is techno night. Stay here for a minute, I need to go grab Larry. I wonder how they got in here tonight?"

In the short time I've been chatting with Marco, he's explained to me the entire employee dynamic of Club Lotus. Larry is the weekend manager of the club, the younger brother of the owner, and an absolutely no-nonsense prick. Marco doesn't seem to like him very much, but admits that he does a pretty decent job of running the club.

My glass of merlot is beginning to settle in.

All the telltale signs are there.

My lips and tongue are feeling numb, my eyes are becoming a tad more sensitive to the intricate lighting caressing the dance floor, and I have a permanent goofy grin on my face. I'm a little past buzzed but not quite plastered. Amazing. I thought for sure that this third one would set me right on my ass. Maybe I'm building up a wine tolerance; which I guess isn't something necessarily to brag about.

As I bob my head to the rapid-fire beat of the latest song, I can't help but watch the scene unfold out of the corner of my eye towards the end of the bar. The woman Marco mentioned, a strikingly beautiful blond woman with a horrendously tacky turquoise colored dress on is arguing with an average-looking redhead. The redhead has on a pair of ultra-skinny jeans (way too small for her) and some sort of weird, retro flowered top. Both women are clearly out of their element. Their clothes seem really cheap and overall they just appear to be oddly out of place. Even more so than myself or beer boy. At least I dressed the part tonight with Sloan's help.

The music is blasting entirely too loudly for me to understand what is being said, but sometimes you need not hear the actual words to understand what is transpiring between two people. If I had to guess, I'd say that they were "frenemies" for some ridiculous reason that goes way back to high school, and that they were looking for any excuse to argue with each other. A couple of drinks and loud music have a way of creating an atmosphere ripe with negative possibilities. In this case, it was a high possibility that someone was going to get their face smashed in. My money was on the redhead.

I spot Marco talking to Larry, and then the two of them start fast-walking towards the two women. It was actually hysterical, because I don't think I've ever seen two men walking across a club with arms and elbows pumping like that. I decide right then that Marco more than likely likes boys and was in no way flirting with me earlier, unless the wine is making me a little judgey.

As if everything is unfolding in front of me like a movie in slow motion, I continue to watch the two women arguing. The level of their voices seems to rise as I watch their facial expressions grow increasingly animated and contorted. I still can't make out what they are saying, but the one with the itsy-bitsy jeans on starts moving closer and closer towards the other woman's face.

I whip my head back towards my right and watch as Larry and Marco continue to move toward the scene, trying to draw as little attention to themselves as they can, but also trying to get to the girls as quickly as possible. Larry's eyes seem to now be fixated on one particular point. The beautiful blond's lap. I watch as she reaches into her silver clutch, which is lying across her lap, and she pulls out what looks like a set of clunky car keys.

Thanks to the wine, I am still swaying and bobbing in my seat to the pulse of the music as the entire scene plays out. The music basically serves as a soundtrack for the drama unfolding in front of me. I am just waiting for the first punch. I know it's brewing. I can see it in itsy-bitsy's eyes. Like I said, my money was on her.

Larry and Marco are sprinting across the club at this point. Gently elbowing their way through the writhing bodies on the dance floor, making their polite "excuse me's" as they do. I'm not really sure why they are so frantic about reaching the two women. No blows have been thrown yet, and as far as I can tell, it all seems to be a lot of loud name-calling and neck rolling. Total girl shit.

And that's when it happens.

Pure pandemonium.

ELIZABETH

I AM CHOKING AND GASPING for breath. The surrounding air is thick and heavy. Tears pool in the corners of my eyes, because the burning sensation of the chemicals is so overpowering. I reactively blink and squeeze my eyelids tightly to stop the stinging, but all that does is give me a dull headache at my temples.

I'm not sure what to do with my hands first, as I indecisively alternate between rubbing the corners of my eyes and grasping at my throat, almost breaking the delicate gold chain hanging around my neck. I desperately need fresh air, but my lungs are being denied what they crave most and like the idiot I am, I have paid no attention to where the exit doors are located. This is exactly what I deserve for not listening to my inner voice. My instincts. My gut. The voice that told me to just keep my ass at Sloan's, eat ramen, and watch Netflix.

Panic swells inside of my chest. Was it those girls that did this? Although I know that a little pepper spray never killed anyone, I am also well aware of the pandemonium that spraying it in a confined location can cause. I wonder if people feel this type of dread right before they meet death, like in the final five seconds before a fatal car collision or a plane crash.

While I can't see very much, especially at a distance, I can definitely hear the quickening click-clack sounds of women's stilettos and the growing chant of deep male voices straining the words, "Push! Push!" in unison.

After a few high-pitched screams, I realize that the surrounding hysteria is starting to mushroom, and I am certain that the shrieks are coming from young women being pushed and crushed not only at the front doors but through the other exit side doors as well. Without consideration of others, people are running, pushing, and stepping on top of other people's bodies to get out of the club as fast as they can.

Not. Good. At. All.

The level of danger in the room is rising at an accelerated pace, and I realize that I need an exit plan and fast, because getting out of the club through the main doors unscathed doesn't seem to be in my immediate future. I don't see her at first, but am relieved when Sloan grabs me from behind by the shoulders. "It's me, Bitsy."

"Thank God," I exhale.

Sloan coughs a bit while spitting out her idea of an exit plan. "We'll get trampled if we stay by the bar or if we try to leave now. Let's hide behind the speaker over there. When it thins out, we'll leave."

"I can't breathe," I say, and frankly I don't really like her exit strategy.

Hide in the middle of a chemical apocalypse? So at this point I am freaking out, but I also don't have any other better ideas, especially with the three drinks I've consumed clouding any coherent judgment I have left.

Since I don't want to compound the issue by totally losing it, I take a few deep yoga breaths (not easy since the air is filled with pepper spray), while I continue to consider her suggestion. I can feel Sloan carefully studying my face. She knows I'm on the verge of a meltdown.

"I can't see the exit, Bitsy," she explains slowly to me like I'm an idiot. "But I definitely hear people getting mashed. Trust me, the best thing to do is to wait this out. We'll be fine. Take shallow breaths and hold on to me." She pats my shoulder in an attempt to calm me. I'm pretty sure she can see the fear all over my face and oozing out of my pores. I hate who I've become since that night. I reluctantly offer a soft, "ok" in agreement and follow her lead. Both of us moving low to the ground.

Sloan's plan to get us out of the club in one piece includes having us, much to my horror, crawl on all fours to hide behind a huge sound speaker that I pray is unplugged or blown out, so that I'll still have my hearing by the end of the night. In my favorite and only pair of two-hundred-dollar jeans, a halter top, and platform heels we start our trek towards the speaker by crawling our way across the gritty, sticky, concrete floor of one of the most exclusive clubs in the city. Or so I've been told.

Sloan turns her head. "Don't stare at my ass. I'm going on a Paleo diet on Monday."

I grin at the fact that Sloan is either trying desperately to make me laugh or that she's extremely delusional. There is nothing fat about her ass. I wish I had that ass.

As we hesitantly creep across the floor of the club, we discover all sorts of disgusting surprises with the palms of our hands. Flattened pieces of chewing gum, small puddles of beer, droplets of wine, bits of paper, grit and dirt. Really gross stuff and somewhat surprising considering where we were, plus it wasn't even that late yet. How can all this crap be on the floor already? I just pray to myself that no one has spit on the floor.

That would be IT for me.

"I can't believe this nonsense." Sloan stops crawling for a moment, still slightly coughing. "I can't believe I paid a hundred bucks a piece for this."

Sloan mentioned in the cab ride over that there was a pretty steep cover charge to get inside the semi-exclusive club, but that there were always plenty of attractive men inside to buy us drinks to offset the cost. Her words, not mine. She didn't tell me how much the cover charge was, because she was treating me to a night out to cheer me up. Plus, she makes a lot of money selling some sort of generic version of Viagra to doctors.

Two hundred bucks for a night out is normal for her, but regardless of that, she's right. This is nonsensical. Who pays through the nose for a night out only to end up having to scramble around on the floor like we're in the middle of some drunken frat party?

I nod my head in agreement and agree with her. "Yep, this is really dumb."

We finally make it to our destination and crouch behind the gargantuan black sound speaker. Luckily the sound seems to have been cut by the deejay, so I'm relieved that we will at least still have our hearing when this is all over. I decide that it won't hurt to say a little silent prayer to myself, and that God will forgive the fact that it is something that I haven't done in a long while.

Between the pepper spray burning my eyes, the drinks fogging my brain, and the sounds of pure terror all around me, I'm getting pretty close to losing it. Someone is definitely going to get hurt tonight. I just hope like hell it isn't me. I can't afford another hospital visit.

As if on cue, in the middle of my "amen," I hear a very clear and distinct set of heavy footsteps advancing towards us. Whoever it is, isn't panicked like the rest of us. He or she (no, it was definitely a he) is moving calmly and very deliberately towards our direction.

I experience a brief moment of alien-like movement in my stomach, warning me of something. I'm not sure what. Maybe to be on guard, or perhaps to run. Suddenly I feel five very warm, strong, and calloused fingers grasp my upper left arm and pull me up on my feet.

"Stand up," the deep voice orders with a rumble. His lips just inches away from my ear. His breath smells of peppermint, chocolate, and cognac. A yummy mixture. It's familiar. Reminds me of Christmas.

His distinctive voice reverberates throughout my body, from the top of my head to the tips of my toes, and then settles in as if making a home in between my legs. I'm shocked at my body's reaction and frankly embarrassed. Typically, I would never blindly follow the commands of a stranger, but this isn't a usual circumstance I find myself in. So for once I decide not to overthink things (like he may be a serial killer) and instead just follow his lead.

With his hand still firmly clasping my upper arm, he notices that my feet are unsteady and quickly adjusts himself to place his other hand loosely around my middle to balance me as I stand. His massive hand almost spans the entire length of my torso and although my clothing serves as a barrier, to me it feels like I have nothing on. His thumb nearly grazes my breast, which sends my nipples into a hard alert, while his pinky finger comes dangerously close to the waistband of my panties.

I am so overwhelmed by all the sensations of him touching me, that my body probably feels heavy to him, as I inadvertently sway slightly forward and allow him to bear more of my weight. My heaviness doesn't seem to be an issue though, as he effortlessly guides me upwards onto my feet with one sweeping movement.

"Easy," he murmurs softly by my ear.

Even with all hell breaking loose in the club, that one word, the stranger's raspy voice, and his unforgettable hands are all I can concentrate on. His touch feels personal, careful, and intimate, as if we already know each other or as if we are definitely about to. As he continues to direct me, his commands suddenly turn somewhat clipped, almost like he is annoyed with me for some unknown reason.

"She with you?"

"Yes."

"Grab her hand too."

"Wait, I-" I protest. His terse tone throwing me off.

"Grab her," he orders again.

As he continues to hold on to me, to help me keep my balance, I reach down to grab Sloan's arms and lift her up with me. "Come on, Sloan."

"Walk," is all the stranger says next.

And we do.

I trust that he knows where he is going, because I still can't see much. Between the pepper spray up my nose and all the wine that I had earlier, standing up so quickly makes me feel a little light-headed. I've been rubbing my eyelids and contact lenses for about ten minutes, but now they are feeling like little dry circles of sandpaper scraping against my pupils, so I decide to just pluck them out and toss them as we walk.

Things will be fuzzy until I get home, but that's better

than the permanent scars I will have on my corneas if I left the little suckers in any longer. It's actually a really gross thing to do since there isn't enough Purell in the entire state of Pennsylvania to get my hands clean from crawling across the floor of a nightclub, but I just don't really seem to care at this point.

Without saying another word, we walk for about seventy-seven more steps (yes I count the steps, because I do weird counting things like that when I'm terribly nervous) further into the club and then down a short corridor, until I feel a sharp gust of cool evening air blow on my face. The breeze feels absolutely life affirming. That's when I know that we must be close to an exit. We're actually going to make it out of here. I just hope that we have reached an exit door that we won't get trampled walking through.

The stranger positions Sloan and I in front of him as we continue to push our way through the door. When two guys dressed in button-down shirts and dark slacks walk swiftly towards us and start pushing us roughly from the side, it takes the stranger only several seconds to wrap one of his massive palms around one of the guys' throats.

"Step the fuck back," he growls, and then both of them jump back as high and fast as two high school cheerleaders.

"Sorry, man," one of them mumbles.

We finish elbowing our way out the set of steel double doors in front of us, with the stranger's help of course, and I'm actually wondering why there aren't more people at this exit. I really want to round back and tell some people inside about the exit doors over here, but I know that Sloan would try to fight me first, before she would let me go back inside Armageddon. And I'm thinking this guy wouldn't let me do it either.

"Don't stop. We're crossing the street," the deep voice

orders while expertly guiding me across the street with his hand ever present on the exposed small curve of my back.

The halter top Sloan loaned me gives him easy access, and so with every step I take, my entire body can't help but be laser focused on the spot where his warm hand rests. I don't want to obsess about it, but I can't help it.

Once the three of us make it to the other side of the street, I bend myself over at the waist and rest my hands on my knees, silently grateful for the crisp midnight air that's seeping up my nostrils and down my throat. Utterly relieved that I made it safe and sound out of another life-threatening situation ... again. I must have a guardian angel watching over me or a mischievous one who enjoys tormenting me.

"Take a few deep breaths, but slowly," the stranger directs both of us while still only touching me. Is he ever going to stop touching my back? It's driving me bat shit crazy.

Finally, I begin to feel some actual relief from the burning sensations of the pepper spray, and my skin and eyes feel better as well. As I stand to a full stretch with my palms clasped together, inside out and above my head, my lungs delightfully fill again with oxygen and then...

I freeze.

FOUR

ELIZABETH

I THINK I HEAR SLOAN asking me with worry in her voice if I've bumped my head, but she could be speaking Greek to me right now, because at this moment I am face to face with the most intimidating set of beautiful midnight black eyes I have ever seen.

They are bottomless, and they move and dance like dark pools of liquid ink. Once those deep-set eyes lock intently on mine, they render me what could be embarrassingly described as "stuck on stupid," because a million thoughts are racing through my mind (mostly dirty ones), which fortunately for me, I am unable to communicate.

I can't talk.

I can't smile.

I can barely breathe.

He's wearing a suit jacket, and not just any jacket, but what looks to be a custom tailored, midnight blue, very expensive looking one with a white Henley shirt underneath, dark jeans that fit him like a glove, and a pair of black Doc Martens. I notice part of an intricate, black tattoo that I imagine swirls and trails from God knows where, all the way up to the side of his neck. What's visible to the eye is the very curved tip of the tattoo, teasing me as it peeps out from the top of the round collar.

He looks hard and strong, but not steroid beefy, and stands well over six feet tall (my guess is 6'2"), with a broad back and shoulders, a narrow waist and sleek, diamond cut biceps flexing through his suit jacket. He wears his jet-black hair in a very short buzz cut and looks like a badass who reluctantly dressed up for a night out at the club.

Still mute; I quietly drink more of him in.

I am even more drawn to this man's imperfections, because they make him unmistakably beautiful, as well as a lot more interesting than any other man I've ever seen in my life. Most noticeably, the rather wide and deep crescent-shaped scar under his left eye, which I decide to create a story about in my head (which I do often) on how I think he managed to acquire it.

Definitely from a fight. A fight that he won, of course, because he looks like he hasn't lost a fight since he was about twelve years old. If even then. Adding to his appeal is his strong angular jaw and a nose that looks like it may have been broken once or twice, sort of like a boxer's or a hockey player's, as well as the one deep dimple in his left cheek.

One amazing frackin' dimple.

His magnetic, black sable colored eyes are so deep and intense as they trace the lines of my face, I feel as if I could fall into them and end up somewhere in the land of Oz. He looks weathered, and frightening, and delicious all at the same time. The air seems to have been completely sucked out of the atmosphere, and I feel like I'm going to throw up, but in a good way–if that's even remotely possible.

"You all right?" the stranger asks while softly running two of his knuckles along the side of my face.

I nod my head up and down, speechless from his touch. "You okay?" he turns to ask Sloan.

Sloan looks a little green around the gills, but unlike me is able to find her voice.

"Yes–I just need a minute, thank you. You ok, Bitsy?" She asks me with one eyebrow raised. I can tell that she's trying to communicate with her eyes for me to, "get my shit together" in front of this man. This god. This man-god.

But that's Sloan. Confident and cool under pressure. Even under duress, she still manages to look absolutely flawless. With her modern, auburn-dyed pixie cut which pops against her creamy caramel colored skin, God-given size D breasts, and a killer smile; for a moment I'm worried that the stranger is going to realize that he has his hand on the back of the wrong girl. Any given night of the week if we're hanging out, I'm Sloan's "wingman", never the main chick.

Don't get me wrong, I'm not a slouch by any stretch, but I'm also a realist. I'm attractive, but like most women, there are things that I wouldn't mind changing about myself. Like maybe the size of my very wide bell-shaped hips and probably my big hair. Sloan on the other hand doesn't need to change a thing. Heads turn when she enters a room. Men fall all over themselves to buy her a drink. She's Top Model beautiful and typically gets major attention when we hang out.

So I'm kind of confused as to why the stranger doesn't seem to be as interested in her as most men are. But I guess the bigger question is, why do I even care about this? This is part of what's wrong with me. I worry about all the wrong things sometimes. I should just be happy that I've made it out of Club Lotus alive and with 20/20 vision. Not concern myself with who the man-god is interested in. Hell, my boyfriend just dumped me two-seconds ago. I need to stay clear of all men. Especially ones like him.

"I'm good," I assure the two of them.

But I'm not good.

The stranger keeps staring at me in a way that is so electrically charged, that I am sure my skin feels hot to the touch. Flushed. I look away, because I feel like a colony of bats are swarming around in my gut. Blindly banging around inside my body like they're trying to find a way out but can't. I reluctantly look back up to meet his deep-set eyes as he moves a few steps forward and gently lifts my chin with his strong, calloused pointer finger. It's like he knows that there is something else that I want or need to say.

"Thank you," I manage to fumble out softly. "You know, for helping us out of there."

He grins in what I assume is a, "you're welcome" but says nothing. He just keeps staring at me.

Hard.

Sloan lets out an obvious fake cough to break the tension between us, but I am too flustered for it to do much good. My attention waffles between shifting my eyes from the stranger's perfectly shaped lips, to his ears, to the small mole on his neck, to the tip of his tattoo and everywhere else to avoid those eyes of his; clearly calculating every breath I take. I have a deep suspicion that if I stare into his eyes long enough, that he could tell me to jump off of the nearest bridge and I gladly would.

"Tell me your name." His tone has shifted. It seems more urgent and darker.

Suddenly I begin to nervously coil a few strands of my shoulder length hair around my fingers. I don't have a vast amount of experience with guys, but I know with great certainty that I'm in way over my head with this man.

He looks hard and seasoned, like he's been around the block a few times, but in the best way possible. Every woman that walks by is gawking at him, and I imagine that most women are drawn to him like moths to a flame. Clearly, I'm no better, since it's glaringly obvious that the stranger has the unique super power to turn me into a complete moron. I have yet to say one intelligent thing in his presence so far. It's ridiculous. I graduated on the Dean's List for goodness sake.

He reaches over to untangle the hair that I have unwittingly twined around my fingers and then moves forward to tuck the loose strands gently behind my ear. As his fingertips lightly brush the small area of skin behind my ear, I slowly blink my eyes and struggle for shallow breaths. His strong fingers move to raise my chin in order to refocus my attention on him, and when my eyes meet his gaze this time, my body betrays me in a most unmerciful way.

My nipples tighten underneath my flimsy halter top and are on full alert, like a pair of headlights. I don't know how he knew to take a look, but the stranger takes a sweeping glance at them, takes a small swipe of his bottom lip with his tongue, and smiles suggestively at me. That tongue move of his makes me wonder what it would feel like if he touched my taut nipples with those strong fingers and then next with that beautiful mouth. I bet it's deliciously warm and wet.

So as if it isn't enough that I am completely embarrassed by the fact that I've allowed a complete stranger to touch me twice, not to mention my body's response to his handling of me-- I've completely forgotten what his original question was.

I feel seriously discombobulated.

This is six degrees of all kinds of wrong.

"I'm sorry. What did you say?" I ask, annoyed with myself.

While I manage to somehow articulately ask him to repeat the question, I squirm while waiting to hear it repeated, as he lazily rakes his eyes from my neck, to my breasts, to my hips, legs, and then back up to my eyes. When he is finished eye fucking me, he smirks as if I'm already smoking a post-coital cigarette, and then he speaks to me in a way that requires a definite response.

"Your name."

Oh, that's right moron.

"Elizabeth."

He flashes a delicious small grin on his face, which showcases his gorgeous dimple, and I am actually pleased with myself that I was responsible for putting it there.

Oh. My. God. What is my problem?

"Were you having a good time tonight, Elizabeth?"

"In the club? Sure, it was all right." Why does he say my name like that? Dripping in seduction. Like we've already done something very wicked with each other.

"Did you two come together or did you come alone?" he asks with mild curiosity.

"Together," Sloan interjects.

This is the first time I notice that Sloan is staring at the stranger in almost the same way I am. Lustfully. He is sexy as hell; there is no disputing that. I can't even blame her, although I'm starting to not really like it.

"Is this your first time?" He smiles when he asks me that. I assume he is talking about visiting the club, but the question is loaded with sexual innuendo.

"I'm a regular," Sloan interjects again. "But it was her

first time."

I'm not exactly sure what's going on here. Sloan is acting strangely. I need her to shut up and stop speaking for me. I can't believe that I'm even considering this, but is it possible that she could be a little miffed that the stranger isn't giving her the usual attention she receives from men? Or maybe she's just being a good friend and answering for me, since I seem to be incapable of talking for myself. It's probably the latter. That's what I choose to think, anyway.

"Is that right–" He holds his finger up and turns his back to us to take a call on his cell phone. "Excuse me one second, ladies."

"Yes." I hear him answer gruffly to the person on the phone. "It's done."

Still feeling slightly shell-shocked and buzzed from a combination of everything that has taken place over the course of the evening, I stop trying to eavesdrop on the stranger's phone call, and glance across the street towards the entrance of the club in disbelief. What a strange night.

I see small clusters of men and women in assorted states of disarray. Some people were clearly hurt and nursing wounds from being nearly trampled. Others were hunched over making calls on their cells or sitting on the ground coughing and rubbing their eyes, which were no doubt still smarting from the pepper spray. The police have finally arrived and have started the business of clearing the club, tending to the injured, and questioning staff.

I scan the crowd to look for Marco, but notice someone else. The same blond from the bar who was wearing the really cheap looking, tacky off the shoulder turquoise mini dress with ruching on the side. She's a very pretty girl but was dressed and acted like she didn't know it. She was also the woman who I suspected to be the cause of this entire evening from hell. I'd bet someone a hundred dollars that she had a bottle of pepper spray attached to those keys that she pulled out in the club. In fact, I was pretty sure that I saw her pull it out and press the button, although it is hard to say for sure due to my vantage point at the bar. I wonder if the police have questioned her yet.

I watch her reservedly as her eyes squint in my direction and then hone in on the person speaking on his cell phone directly behind me. The same man who was responsible for commanding my nipples to attention just moments ago. He notices her staring at him too and abruptly finishes his call. At least it seems abrupt to me, but maybe that's his usual phone etiquette.

When he walks back over and stands directly in front of me, I don't like how completely out of my own body I feel. I bravely look up into his eyes, thinking maybe the words will come, but now I wish I hadn't. My breathing slows and my chest locks up. His eyes are like magnets. Pulling me into some strange vortex. I've read novels featuring characters that have an instant attraction to each other, and I roll my eyes every time I read one of those plots. I've been attracted to several guys over the years, and seriously dated two of them, but experienced nothing like this. I didn't think this really existed.

"Are you sure you're okay?" he asks with concern.

"Yes." I nod while rubbing my arms.

"Cold?"

I can't hide the fact that I'm slightly shivering. The nights are getting cooler as the summer winds down, not to mention the fact that I'm totally underdressed. Last time I'll wear Sloan's skimpy tops.

"A little."

He takes off his jacket and wraps it around my shoulders, allowing his hands to linger across my shoulders a little longer than necessary. The lining of his jacket is a midnight blue satin, which smells uniquely like him, and it warms me quickly with his residual body heat. I was just about to let out a small audible groan, as if I hadn't caught myself. I'm pretty sure he notices.

He pushes up the sleeves of his shirt and holy mother of god there are more tats. Two intricate arm sleeves worth on strong, corded forearms. A simple but very expensive looking silver watch adorns his left wrist. I can't help but stare, and once again, he notices.

"May I ask what you do?" he asks.

"What I do?" I nervously rub the thin horizontal gold bar necklace I'm wearing between my fingers.

"Most of the women that come to the club on techno night are tightly wound corporate types looking to let loose."

"And I don't look like the corporate type?" I take slight offense. Why, I'm not sure.

"I know you're not one of those types."

"I work in the tech industry." He nods his head. "Interesting." "What do you do?" I ask.

"I'm a consultant."

With all those tattoos? I highly doubt that.

"Can I give you a ride home?"

"Umm, no we're fine." Right now, almost every man looks like a potential drug addict or drug dealer to me. Including him. Especially him.

"Well, he could drop us off–" Sloan adds her two cents, but I quickly cut her off.

"We're. Fine," I state firmly.

"Sheesh. It's not like we live that far, Bitsy." Sloan mutters under her breath like a bratty teenager whose mom just scolded her.

She's definitely annoyed with me, but it's been a long night, and it's just dawned on me that I still don't know the stranger's name. I was too dumbstruck to remember to ask him, and he never offered it.

This is just one of the many obvious red flags waving directly in front of my face about how lost I could become in a man like this. An attraction like this. I barely escaped the last relationship I thought I was so careful with. I'm definitely not doing that again. So I listen to my mind and not my hormone driven body. If I accept a ride home or go anywhere with this guy, I may just barely survive it.

Do I think he's a serial killer? No. But do I think he is someone with the capability of destroying me nonetheless. Absolutely. No, thank you.

I finally see a yellow cab that looks empty and raise my hand to hail it. I slip the stranger's jacket from around my shoulders and hand it back to him. It's so weird that I feel like I've lost something important when I give it back. I already miss his scent and his warmth. Sloan jumps in the cab's backseat and gives me a moment while I say my good-byes to him.

"Thank you again for everything tonight," I say sincerely.

He nods silently at me with an expressionless look on his face as he holds the door for me. I hope my refusal of a ride didn't offend him. Not that it matters. I'll never see him again. Once I'm inside the cab, I exhale the breath that I have been holding, and that's when he thumps the hood of the car twice, signaling for the cab driver to drive away.

As we pull away, I turn my head like a child to watch him through the back window; and as his silhouette grows smaller in the distance, my body weeps for the many orgasms that will never be.

FIVE

ROMAN

SUNLIGHT STREAMS IN THROUGH an unfamiliar window, warming my face, and I'm pissed about it. I just need twenty more damn minutes of sleep. Just twenty. Grumbling profanities, I pull the sheet over my head to block the sun's rays and notice a pair of bare oversized breasts close to my chin. They are beautiful, perky, round globes that no doubt have been perfected by a surgeon's skilled hands; but I have no fucking idea who they belong to, even though they were in my mouth not less than five hours ago.

Doesn't matter. It never matters. I'm not built in a way that it would ever matter.

A month or so ago, a woman whose name is escaping me at the moment, gave me remarkable head and got so upset that I was disrespecting her like some two-dollar whore, because I got up to leave as soon as she wiped her mouth. She told me I committed a "hit and run" and that I was trying to leave the scene of a crime without exchanging information, which was a major offense. I'm not kidding. She used those exact damn words. Did I mention that this woman was in the police academy? (I went through a phase of law and order types.) So shutting all that down, I swiftly cuffed her ass to the headboard and fucked her hard doggy style while calling out each number of my cell phone with each punishing stroke.

Over and over and over.

Funny thing was that she never did quite remember the number. I guess it's kind of difficult to concentrate when your eyes are rolling back inside of your head. I'd say it was a win-win for both of us.

The woman I'm lying next to right now doesn't seem to mind a little hit and run. I can tell that she is awake based on her breathing pattern, although she's pretending to be asleep. It's rare that I hook up with someone who is embarrassed about the night's sexual escapades, so it must be that she's as anxious for me to leave, as I am to go. Maybe she has a boyfriend. I don't give a shit. This was a mistake anyway.

I just needed something to help me clear my head of all things Elizabeth. The woman I spotted immediately as she entered The Lotus. The woman I couldn't keep my eyes off of all night. As I watched her (more like stalked her), a foreign vibration snaked through my chest that was new and powerful and alarming. Threatening to choke the ever-living shit out of me.

I think it was ... possession.

I watched Elizabeth like a hawk as she ordered and drank three glasses of red wine, danced like no one was watching, flirted with a bartender who is on my short list to beat the fuck up next time I see him, and then as she almost got herself trampled.

Alcohol isn't helping me forget her, so I thought maybe pussy would. It's been a week, but I can still see her sexy ass curves, feel her soft hair, smell her. Like cinnamon and sunshine. It's an attraction I don't begin to even understand, nor do I want to explore. I can't remember the last time that I thought about the same woman for over seven days.

Wait ... maybe because it's been never.

I glance out of the mystery woman's bedroom window and realize based on the age and architecture of the buildings surrounding me that I'm clear across town. I'm going to need a little extra time to make it to my morning meeting. A meeting that I called.

Shit.

An incoming text vibrates my phone to life. With one eye open, I scan the surrounding area for my cell. It's in the bed, tangled in the sheets.

Jade: The old man is waiting.

Double shit.

Me: Stall for me.

Jade: Long night?

Me: Mind your business

Jade: I'll give you a $100 if you can tell me her name:)

Me: I'll give you a $1000 if you quit.

Jade: Give me $10,000 and you have a deal.

Me: Just stall. I'll fire you later.

My clothes are strewn all over the floor of what's her name's bedroom floor. I'm not really sure what that's about since I'm not typically a rip my clothes off in the heat of passion kind of guy. That's some soap opera shit. Mostly because passion is for pussies in love. I don't do passion, and I damn sure don't do love. I fuck. And that doesn't require a whole lot of demonstrative hoo-hah. Just technique. Which I have plenty of.

As I pick my jeans up and yank them back on, what's

her name's body shifts and stretches as if she's finally waking up, when I know good and damn well that she's been awake for hours. What theatrics.

Then, regretfully, she speaks.

"Hey good morning," she says with a somewhat scratchy deep voice. She must be a smoker, and I must have been really drunk to miss that. I don't like smokers. Especially when they're sticking their tongues down my throat.

"I added my number to the contacts in your phone. It's under–"

"Why?" I demand to know flatly.

I swear that I'm not purposely trying to be an ass, okay maybe I am, but I'm annoyed that she was handling my phone while I was sleeping; and I'm even angrier that I was sloppy enough to spend the night here and not have my passcode on. I've got to ease up on the Jack Daniels. I'm slipping.

"In case you want to call me."

"I won't," I say, sitting on the edge of the bed, pulling my t-shirt over my head, with my back still turned to her.

Just gotta find my boots, and I'm out of here.

"You may change your mind."

When she sits up and the sheet falls, I turn my head and get a good look of her entire body. She's definitely my usual type. Big perky boobs. Flat stomach. Slender hips. Extremely long legs. Plus, she knows she looks good. Confidence is always attractive, but that changes nothing. We're both grown, and this was what it was. "I don't do second dates," I tell her honestly.

She pauses for a moment. "What ... Why?"

"Not interested in more than once."

She served her purpose. Well ... then again, maybe she didn't. The whole point was to use this chick's body to forget another woman's. But that shit didn't work, because all I seem to be thinking about is the woman who is not my usual type, clear as day.

Elizabeth's petite, soft, curvy ass body in those tiny jeans. Hugging her hips and ass so sweetly. That barely-there halter accentuating her rounded shoulders and those heavy tits and tight nipples. Damn.

She points her finger at me. "I heard you were a world class jerk. In fact—"

"Did you come?" I abruptly interrupt her, because I could give two shits what she heard about me from whatever club skanks she rolls with.

"What—"

"I asked if I made you come last night."

She turns her lips up. "Yes, but—"

"Did I disrespect you at all?"

"No, but you—"

"So, let's be clear. I made you come. Loud, hard, and more than once if I recall. I'm pretty sure I even said goodnight; the polite motherfucker that I am. We slept, and now it's a new day, and I have to go. If you're going to fuck strangers who you take back to your apartment, then you're going to have to toughen up. Not everyone is going to want to go steady afterwards."

What's her name was finally stunned and silent.

Just the way I like 'em.

SIX

ROMAN

"WELL, LOOK WHO THE CAT drug in?" Jade quips with that smart-ass mouth of hers. Her delicate heart-shaped lips would be sort of appealing, if I didn't look at her like anything more than an annoying little sister and a competent assistant.

I admit that I look like shit.

I need a shower and a shot of something in my coffee, but I don't have time for all of that before I meet with the old man. Joseph's going to want to be assured that I have things handled.

"Is that how you greet the man who's paying your rent?" I kid with Jade.

"You pay my salary, not my rent," she says as she hands me a fresh cup of black coffee.

"Potato, potahto."

The door to the conference room shoots open and two mounds of muscle who closely resemble each other barge into the room.

"The King brothers are here!" The younger, louder one named Cutter yells out like the town crier. "Knucklehead,"

I respond, giving him a strong hug and handshake combination.

I give a simple head nod to the other brother, Camden, as he takes a seat in one of the large conference chairs by the window. His body language speaks volumes. He's all about business today and is trying to exude an air of dominance in the room. He's getting mentally prepared for Joseph, my father, someone who is not one of his favorite people right now.

"Boys," Jade greets them with a smirk.

"Hey," they both reply in unison. "Wassup Jade."

The King brothers and I work for my father and the company, which he founded, Masterson & Associates (us being the associates). We are for lack of a better word "fix-ers." We spend our days getting spoiled celebrities and other wealthy people out of trouble, and that's a messier job than you would imagine. Not slick and glamorous like that chick on the television show Scandal made it look.

Jade works as a sort of an all-purpose assistant for the three of us, which basically means that she keeps us on point and runs interference between the three of us and my father a lot.

When I met her, we were teenagers, and she was getting beat up on a regular basis by her low-life ex who was addicted to painkillers and using her to fund his habit. She loved him, but thankfully she loved herself more, and didn't go back to him after I beat the hell out of his high ass. I don't have a lot of patience for addicts, probably because of my mommy issues, but that's another story for another day. Jade and I have been friends ever since. In fact, she is probably one of my only true friends. Her and the Kings.

"You look like shit on a stick," Cutter says to me while laughing heartily.

"What did you tell him?" I ask Jade to purposely ignore Cutter's observation. "Where did he go?"

"Where did who go?" The cool as ice voice asks from the doorway.

With my back towards the all too familiar voice, I walk around to the buffet table to grab a handful of M&Ms out of a plain and slightly dented silver candy dish.

"Morning, Joseph," I say half-heartedly to my father as a I loosely shake a few of my favorite candies in my fist then pop them into my mouth one by one.

"Morning? It's damn near the afternoon. Why are you late, Roman? I believe you called this meeting."

Standing tall with a stern look in his eyes, even at my age, my father still intimidates me. His salt and pepper hair and impeccably tailored three-piece suit make him appear quite formidable, and of course I've seen firsthand the rage that simmers behind that cool exterior of his. Jade quietly leaves the room as she always does when we have meetings, unless the old man requests her to stay.

"Had some stuff come up," I say coolly.

"Stuff," he repeats flatly, as if he's annoyed.

I'm used to his disapproval, though. Joseph hates the fact that no matter how successful he is and how much money he makes, that I still sound like everyone from the old neighborhood. Full of excuses, he says. Our old neighborhood, and the people in it, is a place he would very much like to forget. Me, not so much. No matter how much money I make, I always want to remember where I come from. Unlike Joseph, I've never been ashamed of it.

Camden keeps a close but quiet eye on the old man as he smoothes his tie and takes a seat at the conference table.

"I called the meeting to discuss the MTV event, Johnson's DUI, and to also assure all of you that things went smoothly at the club last weekend. We've got Henson right where we want him," I say.

"And where's that?" Camden asks sarcastically.

I really wished what's her name had taken care of my Elizabeth problem, because I'm so fucking wound up by it, that I'm seriously considering beating the crap out of Camden just for being a smartass. I don't need his attitude right now.

"Ready to sign the shittiest ass deal ever and sign over the club like we agreed," I say.

The tension is practically bouncing off the walls of our small conference room. Camden's mood sucks, Cutter is potentially a loose cannon, and I'm not in the mood for anybody's shit. I hope that Camden can see that without me having to spell it out all across his face. We used to wail on each other for fun when we were kids, but we're not those boys anymore. We're grown ass men.

Camden smirks. "You mean the agreement to sign the club over to Joseph here?"

My father rises smoothly to his feet. "Is there something you want to say to me, Camden King?"

I watch Cutter shift in his seat a little. He'll go ape shit if he thinks his brother is being threatened, although that doesn't bother Joseph in the least. He knows I won't let that happen. Regardless of my issues with the old man, he is my father and the boss. I won't let tempers get out of hand.

"I just need it to be crystal clear who and what we're doing all this work for," Camden says.

"You work for me. You have always worked for me. I AM this business, and if you don't want to work for me any longer, all you have to do is say the word. I have no interest in employing unhappy people."

I have considered the fact that there is a small possibility that Camden and Cutter are speaking directly with someone at a competing agency behind my father's back. Few can be trusted in this game, and not everyone can get things done like we can. We rarely fail at what we do, and that's a big commodity in this game. I can see how another agency might assume that the boss's son isn't going to go anywhere, but that perhaps the King brothers could be persuaded to leave Masterson & Associates. I just hope that isn't the case. I have no interest in finding out that two of my oldest (and only) high school friends would be so willing to stab me in the back. I think I'd rather live in ignorance.

"Is that right, Joseph? You care about my happiness? About my brother's happiness?"

Camden is leaning back in the chair with his arms crossed and legs stretched out in front of him. I feel like I'm missing something. I know Joseph gets under his skin sometimes, but now I'm starting to wonder if something else is going on between them.

Joseph squints his eyes at both brothers. "I care as much as I should care about an employee."

Cutter's fists are clenching. He's going to blow if I don't diffuse the situation.

"I'm meeting with Henson in a few hours," I interject. "I need to run if I'm going to look half decent before I get there. We'll talk about the awards show and the DUI later. You're fine with the contract details right, Joseph?"

There's a moment of silence in the room as each man is considering what they are going to say or possibly do next. Joseph smoothes his tie again and turns his head to look at me. I know him. He's giving me the Masterson once over. Observing my body language. Trying to assess if there's anything I'm hiding. I know it well, because I do the same thing to men every day. Sometimes it's so fucking clear where I get my trust issues from. I'm not hiding anything though. I just want him to get the hell out of the room before somebody blows.

"The details are fine. Of course, if you can negotiate less, then do so, but make it look believable. It can't look like a shakedown. We're not mafia or gangsters. We're business owners."

I know all of this already. He's drilled the art of our brand of business negotiation into my head a hundred times, but I still nod my head to him in understanding and respect.

"Got it."

Then I walk over to the safe and get my gun. A five-year-old Beretta that's never failed me yet. While I'm checking the chamber for bullets, Joseph walks up behind me.

"I need to speak with you briefly about family business."

"All right."

I give Camden and Cutter a look that asks them to leave the room, and frankly I'm relieved because that means that I don't have to give Camden my "what the fuck" speech, because I don't feel like giving it, and I sure as shit don't feel like arguing with him. I already get it. What reason would a fixer like Joseph need to own several Philadelphia night-clubs? And why is it our job to make these deals happen for him? He hasn't been paying us extra.

So yes, I get it. Camden feels like we're getting dicked over, and so do I. I'm just not sulking and pouting over it like a twelve-year-old kid. My father can run his business however he wants. It's up to us whether we are going to put up with the terms. That's why when the right opportunity presents itself, I'm going to stop working for him. Stop doing this shit period. I'm not stupid. I know that Joseph has no intentions of passing the business on to me. All I am is a well-paid, glorified henchman. Muscle. The enforcer. Plus, I think the crazy old man intends on living forever.

"Your cousin is coming to live with Juliette and me for a while."

"What cousin?" Joseph doesn't keep in touch with his only brother and my mother has no siblings.

"Juliette's niece. The one you buried up to her eyeballs in dirt when she was just a little girl."

This conversation was boring me to tears. Everything always comes back to Juliette. His sun, moon, and stars. It's nothing personal against her. I like her ... but enough already.

"And?"

"She's in trouble. I don't know the details, because her parents refused to tell Juliette everything, but Juliette is worried sick."

"Is she pregnant?"

"Not that type of trouble. Our type of trouble. I need you to find out what kind exactly, and then I need you to handle it. Nothing messy, Roman. Just handle it. Come by the restaurant early tonight, and I'll introduce you to her."

This is just fucking great. Another non-paying side job for Joseph.

Babysitting, my little cousin.

SEVEN

ROMAN

WHEN I ARRIVE TO THE WORN metal door of Club Lotus, I double check the streets, making sure that Henson doesn't have anyone watching the front of the club. This negotiation will only work if I catch him off guard. I make sure that my sidearm is securely concealed under my jacket, that I have the contract in my hands, and my phone is on vibrate. The door is open and so I immediately walk straight into the big jelly belly of security.

"What do you want?"

"Where's Henson?" I ask the four hundred-pound, bald-headed man giving me the screw face.

"He wasn't expecting you."

"He'll want to talk to me. I'll be at the bar pouring myself a shot of something."

Club Lotus looks like a bomb was set off inside. That's what happens when hundreds of people panic in a closed area. Expensive sound equipment is ruined. Chairs are broken. Tables are on their sides. The floor is littered with glass, napkins, and random things like shoes and lighters.

Doesn't anybody clean up in here? It's been over seven damn days.

I'm reminded of last week when I was sitting in this same corner and spotted Elizabeth as she entered the club. I'd been watching the door all night, because I was waiting for the women I hired to take their positions and begin our very much-orchestrated disruption. I'm not easily distracted from work, especially when it comes to tits and ass, but this was no normal woman.

She didn't belong here.

She didn't seem polished or pretentious, as most of the women here, although she was definitely classy. It was also obvious that she wasn't on the hunt for some dick for the night, like many of the overworked and high-strung young career women who frequented the club.

She was new. It was clearly her first time, and it irked me a little that her friend left her by herself. Men have radar when it comes to that type of shit. I could already see a half-dozen men plotting on her spectacular ass by the time she took the dance floor. Did I mention that I am an ass man?

And then when she closed her eyes and started swaying those hips of hers to the rhythm of the music, I nearly lost my shit. I thought to myself, that if I wasn't on a job, how I'd walk up behind her and slide my hand down the front of her jeans inside her panties. Or maybe she wasn't wearing any panties? Hell, that would be even better.

I'd rub her out right on the dance floor and just wish a motherfucker would say something about it. She'd moan out a plea for me to stop or to not stop right as she climaxed, but that's when I'd turn her around and put my mouth over hers to swallow that orgasm for her and keep it only between us.

I had been way deep inside my fantasy when I noticed some punk kid come up behind her on the dance floor.

Dancing behind her ass, a little too close for my taste. It was almost as if he was in my head and was acting out all the things I wanted to do to her myself.

I swallowed another shot of Jack and gritted my teeth when he placed his palm on the side of her waist. The deep-seated anger that I've been able to carefully keep in check and bring forward only on command was threatening to rise up. That new thing snaking in my chest was constricting my airway. Challenging me to do something about the kid. I tightened my fists as I silently dared the little man-child to touch her just one more time. If he did, I was going to have to come out of the shadows and wring his fucking neck.

It wasn't part of the night's plan though, so I forced myself to calm down. I gave things another minute to play out and relaxed a little when I noticed that the object of my fantasies had it handled. She whispered something in the kid's ear, and he left with his tail between his legs; and fuck if she didn't look sexy as hell when she did it. I had to keep reminding myself that I was there for business, while I silently gawked at the first woman to ever hold my rapt attention.

Ever.

* * *

"Masterson."

"Henson."

Henson was a man in his late forties who had probably spent every dime he had on purchasing and promoting Club Lotus into what it is today. We already knew of each other somewhat because of my presence in other events around the city, and we didn't exactly like each other.

Unfortunately for him, my father had his eyes set on

acquiring Club Lotus and there wasn't much a man like Henson could do about it. He didn't have enough money, and he didn't have enough clout to deal with the likes of Joseph Masterson.

"What do you need?" he asks me stiffly. "As you can see, the club is closed until I can clean this shit up."

"With three women in the hospital due to injuries they sustained here last week, I'd assume you were closed indefinitely. Don't you have Philly PD and every other agency in this city breathing down your neck right now?" I ask smugly.

"You seem to know a lot about my business. Matter of fact, I heard you were in the club that night. I wouldn't be surprised if it was you who set off the goddamn pepper spray."

"Watch your mouth, asshole."

"Then what the hell do you want?"

"I want to help you solve your problem."

"And how would you do that?"

"I have a buyer for the Lotus."

"A buyer?" he asks, as if he's insulted. "I'm not selling."

"You are selling and you know why?"

He's glaring at me, but lets me continue without interruption.

"Because you have no choice. You're going to get sued for what happened in here last week, and I know you don't have the money to pay those women. Your liability insurance has lapsed, and you are barely paying the mortgage on this place as it is. You're also about to lose your liquor license, which as you know will kill your bottom line faster than anything else. My buyer is willing to take on all your debts and all the risk. All you need to do is walk away."

"Walk away with WHAT cocksucker!"

Masterson

"Debt free. Lawsuit free."

Henson sneers. "I need more than my debt cleared to give someone all of this."

"All of what? Look around. Really look Henson. What do you actually have now? Bills. Expenses. Headaches."

Henson looks around the club that he's built over the last five years with sad eyes. In my work there's no room for compassion or pity, so even though his eyes are getting glassy, I don't feel even the smallest pang of guilt for basically robbing him blind. We'd be getting a prime piece of center city real estate for essentially nothing, which is good business 101. Of course we'd have to deal with the inevitable lawsuits headed our way, but Joseph can handle all of that with a phone call. Politicians in this town are notoriously crooked and can easily be bought.

"Who's the buyer?" he asks me what's basically a rhetorical question.

He already knows who my father is and what he's been up to in the real estate scene around the city, but I'll play his game. I down the rest of my shot and slam the shot glass on the counter.

"I'm the buyer's proxy and the offer is up in twenty-four hours. Call me when you're ready. By the way, who was working the door that night?"

Before he answers, he stares at me for a moment, and gives me a look that seems to imply how dare I ask him anything after the shit I just pulled.

"Puma."

He points to the big dude that let me in tonight.

"Remember, twenty-four hours." I say.

"I heard you, asshole."

That's when I know I've got him. He's definitely going to call within the hour.

Puma watches me with great disinterest as I walk towards his direction, but I don't give a fuck. I've decided. If I can't get Elizabeth off my mind, then I need to find her. I made a mistake by letting her get in that cab without tasting her at least once. I need to remedy that shit right now.

"What do you want?" Puma asks in an extra deep voice.

Fat dudes always have to act tough. It's amusing to me. "Last Saturday. I need someone's info."

"A member or a guest?" He looks over to Henson for some sort of sign that it's okay to give me the information I'm asking for.

"A guest."

"I don't have that."

"Why?"

"The members are in a database on the computer in the office. The guests that night were all written in the red book. That book has been long gone. It's missing or destroyed. Can't find it in this mess."

"Wait–she came with a member."

"You know the member's name?"

Damn ... what did she call the skinny chick that night?

"No."

"Then you're shit out of luck, homie."

Oh, for fuck's sake.

EIGHT

ELIZABETH

I STAND NERVOUSLY WITH an awestruck look on my face in front of a massive, pristine, red brick townhouse, while firmly gripping the extended handles of my two over-sized candy-red rolling suitcases. The broad limestone steps and perfectly painted black shutters frame each window and add an additional element of rich original detail to the house. There are two wooden window boxes located on each side of an elegant mahogany front door and each holds an assortment of live begonias–which add a pop of pink color and give the effect of a place that's more lived in instead of one that is simply camera ready. The house has obviously been expensively restored, but it still feels like it's brimming with rich history.

Before I can even place my hand on the brass knocker to announce my arrival, the door jerks open, and there stands a slightly out-of-breath aged version of myself. It's absolutely eerie to see a reflection of yourself in another human being whom you've only briefly talked to on the phone over the holidays. I haven't seen her since I was very young, so in a way, it's like we've never met. I know that I'm supposed to feel some sort of strong connection to her because she's my dad's sister, but the only feeling I can muster up at the moment is reluctant gratitude.

"You're here," she breathlessly declares with one hand on her hip and the other leaning on the doorframe.

"I'm here," I respond with a small smile on my face.

"Please come in, Elizabeth. Welcome home."

My Aunt Juliette is short and curvy with pear-shaped hips just like me. Her skin is flawless and flushed, and her dark hair is pulled back in a sleek ponytail. She is dressed in a pair of black cropped yoga pants and a multi-colored athletic bra. Based on her sweaty appearance, she has obviously been working out, which I find an interesting activity for her to be doing, considering that she knew I would be arriving at this time. I don't know if I should be offended or impressed at her dedication.

I'm originally from Penn-Washington, Pennsylvania. A small suburb outside Philadelphia with tree-lined streets, low taxes, and blue ribbon schools. I've lived in Philly ever since I moved here to attend the University of Pennsylvania as a freshman, but have never visited my aunt the entire time I've lived here.

We don't really know each other, except for the occasional Christmas card or phone call, and this temporary arrangement for me to stay with her has been several phone conversations and countless emails in the making between her and my mother. Not my ideal solution, but I was quickly running out of options. Sloan's place just isn't big enough for the two of us, plus I didn't want to impose myself on her any longer.

I remember flashes of my one and only visit to Aunt Juliette's when I was very young. Now, looking back, I realize that she must have been quite young herself at the time, and that she had just married a man who barely said three words to any of us while we were there.

I didn't understand the dynamics at the time, but for some reason my father was agitated about the visit or maybe about us specifically staying in their home, and I remember him insisting that we sleep on the sofa bed in the living room instead of the guest room that she had all decked out for us. I teared up when I heard my parents arguing about it in the kitchen, but distinctly remember that my father won that battle; so the living room is where we slept.

I remember being excited that I was going to be sleeping between my parents in the living room of such a big, beautiful house. First of all, I'd never slept in anyone's living room before, and secondly, I was thrilled that we were in the "big city" having never left Penn-Washington before. But most importantly, I was grateful that I wouldn't have to sleep anywhere near the boy with the mean eyes who also lived there.

Roman.

When we were first introduced, the dark-haired boy seemed to be as quiet as my new uncle, except for the fact that he stuck his tongue out at me while no one was looking. When I told my mother what he did, she laughed and said that all boys were like that. The next day she forced me to play with him in the backyard while the adults caught up over coffee.

He was a couple of years older than me, so naturally he assumed the role of babysitter, when he was hardly qualified to watch any living thing as far as I was concerned. I was no baby, and he certainly was not the boss of me. What I was though was sheltered, and I never saw his treachery coming.

My aunt's house didn't have a huge backyard like we

did back home, but there was a small patio area in the back with various potted flowers, and a large rectangular patch of grass with a small garden area. Roman explained that Aunt Juliette was planting a small garden of tomatoes, squash, and sunflowers and that he knew a secret to help me grow as well.

"You'll grow as tall as a sunflower," he said. "I know because I helped my friend Peter grow last year. Now he beats everyone in basketball."

I was quite petite when I was a child, so it didn't take a rocket scientist for anyone to figure out that I probably had a strong desire to grow. I could never see much on my tippy toes when we went out to parades or sporting events, because it seemed as if every human being on the planet was taller than me. I hated being short. So it didn't take much for Roman to convince me that if he planted me in the ground, watered me, and we waited, that I'd grow at least three inches by the end of the day.

I believed him.

I was six.

After he handed me a miniature sized gardening shovel, we spent the next fifteen minutes digging the hole together as he told me stories about how he was going to be a professional athlete one day, and how he was going to buy his mom a big house and move in with her when he became rich like his dad. I didn't understand what he was talking about though. I thought my Aunt Juliette was his mother, but I was too excited about the prospect of growing in a day to ask him to explain.

Once the hole was deep enough, Roman told me to jump down in it and he'd fill the hole back up with soil, add a little Miracle-Gro, water me, and wait. Ten minutes later I was buried to my neck in dirt, with the sun beating down on my wet and bushy head of hair with no Roman in sight.

After an hour, I figured I'd grown enough and wanted to get out, but I couldn't move my arms. He'd packed the dirt super tight. In fact, it was almost two hours before my parents and my aunt started looking for us both, assuming that we'd both walked to the playground. When they finally found me, I was in the backyard sunburned, hysterical, and in tears. My father was cussing up a storm as he furiously dug me out.

"I'm getting you out, sweetie, don't worry ... Where the hell is that little juvenile delinquent! Don't worry honey; daddy's going to get you out lickety-split... This is exactly what I'm talking about, Rose. Like father, like son! I'm going to kill that little bastard."

We only stayed another day after that, although we were supposed to stay a week. Tensions were high between the adults, and I refused to speak to Roman for the rest of the visit. Not only did he leave me buried in the yard alone, but I definitely didn't grow. And that made me want to pull his eyelashes out one by one. The little liar.

"Your home is amazing," I say to my aunt while still standing and holding onto my baggage.

"Thank you, sweetie. Gosh, you've grown to be such a beauty, Elizabeth."

"Thanks." I blush.

I think she may attempt to move forward to give me a hug, but I'm not sure. I tensely grip the handles of my luggage as I wait to see what she's going to do. I've never been that big on gestures of affection, but I'm even more skittish since the incident. She notices my discomfort and stops her forward momentum.

"Look at me. I'm a sweaty mess," she giggles in embarrassment. "Why don't you go put your things in your room.

It's the first door on the left at the top of the stairs."

Well, that was awkward and now I feel like crap. It's obvious that I've disappointed her by my knee-jerk reaction.

I can't help but feel bad about it, because she is being so gracious by allowing me to stay here. I know she didn't sign up for housing a twenty-three-year-old she barely knows, and if I know my mother, she probably had a strong hand in this.

"Thanks, Auntie. Oh, just out of curiosity, Roman doesn't still live here, does he?"

My aunt chuckles. "Still holding a grudge, huh? Don't worry about Roman. He has his own place across town. He won't be bothering you. He's not the same mischievous kid he once was, and he only comes by when he has to get work done with Joseph. That's usually during the day. I'm assuming you'll be very busy."

I nod in relief. "Yes, I will."

Thank goodness. I haven't seen that loser in a zillion years, and I have no interest in seeing him again.

You can learn a lot about a person by how they live. My aunt's house is immaculate but not sterile. It's clear that she takes pride in her home and enjoys decorating in warm colors all over the house which makes me think that she is probably a kind and nurturing person.

The first floor is bathed in butterscotch walls and chocolate-colored furniture, with deep red accent chairs and burnt orange pillows. My room is the color of chocolate chip cookie dough, with a sleigh bed and dresser that are both made of a rich brown mahogany wood, and a down comforter and sheets that are all hotel white.

When I rub my hand across the comforter, I can tell

that it's really expensive because of the apparent high thread count. In fact, everything in my room looks like it belongs in the Ritz Carlton or The Four Seasons Hotel. On top of the dresser are only two things. One is a sphere-shaped crystal vase with an arrangement of fresh pink, blue and purple hydrangeas, and the other is a thick, silver framed 5x7 picture of a much younger Juliette holding a big round baby. A baby that looks very much like me. I pick the picture up and examine it closely.

"This baby looks like me," I yell downstairs so that Juliette can hear me.

"Yes, I know." She smiles as she suddenly appears at the doorway of my new bedroom. "You were about six months old there. I loved that age. You were just learning how to sit up on your own and you smiled a lot. So sweet."

"Did you see me a lot when I was a baby?" I ask with surprise.

"Yes," she says in a pained voice. "Before I married your uncle."

"Where were we in this picture?" It doesn't look like her house or even this neighborhood.

"I was visiting a farm in Bucks County about thirty minutes from your house. Some crazy friends of mine bought a farm out there after they got married. They wanted to raise sheep or something. Needless to say, that didn't work out," she chuckles.

"You took me to the farm by yourself?"

"I wanted you to get some fresh air and give your parents a break."

"Was I a difficult baby?" I remember my mom mentioning once or twice that I was colicky.

"Not at all. They were new parents and a bit older. They just needed some downtime. I'm not sure if you know this, but your mother and I were really close once upon a time. She even did my hair and makeup for my prom."

Really?

"Well, what happened between you and Dad?" It's the elephant in the room. I have to ask.

I place the frame back down and start unpacking my things to keep busy, while she contemplates how much of the truth she is going to tell me.

"Does he ever talk about me?"

I notice a small quiver in her voice. I think this may be a bad topic choice for my first hour in my new home. Is she going to cry? Please no.

"No, not really, but to be fair, I never ask him about you."

"Well, it's nothing earth shattering. No big family secret. It's just something that happens in families all the time, I guess. Your father and I were once very close. Much of that changed when I met your uncle."

"Where is Uncle Joseph?" And what does he have to do with their rift, I wonder.

"He's working in his office where he always is."

She quickly changes the subject. "So let's find you something to wear for tonight."

"Tonight?"

"The dinner I'm having for Joseph's birthday. You didn't forget did you?"

Actually, I did. "Oh, I didn't know if that was definitely happening."

"Yes, it is. I hope that's not a problem." "Absolutely not." I try to sound convincing.

"What do you like? Chicken, steak or fish?"

"I'm flexible. Anything is fine."

"I'm going to have all three entrees available then."

Juliette whips out a cell phone the size of my head and swiftly types some sort of note to herself. Probably about the menu.

"I didn't want to overwhelm you your first day here," she continues. "But I've been planning this dinner for months."

"It's fine, Auntie. Really. So what time is this party?" I ask with faux enthusiasm.

"It starts at seven tonight at one of my favorite restaurants," she smiles. "Just a few families and friends."

I pray that Roman won't be there. While I know it's been a hundred years, and we were just kids, my aunt is right. I've been known to hold a grudge. Plus, I heard that the kid has only grown worse with age. I think he even did jail time. At least that's what I overheard my father saying.

"What should I wear?"

I'd always assumed that one issue between my aunt and my dad had something to do with money. My parents did well, but Juliette and my uncle are loaded, and I think my dad may have a problem with it. My father comes from a long line of Philadelphia lawyers, but he is the rebel in the family. Something about not selling out his soul to the establishment, blah, blah, blah.

My father's grandfather, father, and two brothers are all lawyers. Even Aunt Juliette graduated Villanova with a law degree, although to my knowledge she has never used it. But my father ditched law school to become our township's sole courthouse bailiff, where he works every day, never calls out sick, and gets an occasional thrill in stopping local families from getting into fistfights. He loves it, but it isn't exactly what my grandparents consider a profession. To them it is just a mediocre job at best, and I'm sure their disapproval has never set well with my father. No child wants to disappoint their parents.

I'm not exactly sure what Uncle Joseph does, I just know that he owns his own company and makes a shitload of money. So, I'm thinking that maybe my dad and aunt were once close, and when she married my uncle, she for lack of a better term, "sold out." I don't know. Maybe dad just doesn't like him and there is no real reason. I never cared enough in the past to find out the complete story. It wasn't an issue. We never saw them, and I only spoke to Aunt Juliette at Christmas and on birthdays. Maybe I'll find out the actual story now that I live here.

"I don't own anything remotely fancy," I say, hoping to get out of this family party. I'm exhausted and probably a little depressed.

"Anything is fine, Elizabeth. It's a private room. Just family."

Crap to hell, I don't want to go to this. Preparing for this move to my aunt's house has thrown my work schedule completely off, which is horrible when you're a starving entrepreneur. I've decided that my Plan B is going to be an attempt at landing a pitch interview with an investment group that would change everything for me. Sloan briefly dated one of the money managers of the group and promised that she could get me fifteen minutes in front of them.

In order to be ready though, I need to tweak the code to the app and build my database out further. It's important that I dot all my i's and cross my t's. I can't blow this pitch. I may never get an opportunity like it again. But what am I going to tell the woman who's opened her doors to me with no questions asked. That I don't want to go to my uncle's birthday dinner, because I'm an ungrateful brat? "I look forward to it, Aunt Juliette."

"Just call me Juliette, sweetie. I'm not big on formalities."

We both silently stare at each other for an awkward moment. I'm trying to figure us out, and I think that she may be doing the same. We just don't know each other well yet.

"All-righty-then." My aunt breaks the momentary silence between us. "I'll let you get back to it. Can I fix you anything? A sandwich? Maybe a cocktail?"

Do I seem like I need a drink? Probably. It's weird though, having your aunt fix you a drink. Even though I'm totally legal, I would never drink with my parents. I don't care if I'm fifty-years-old and they're eighty-five. Not going to happen.

"I've got vino!" she sing-songs.

Aww, what the hell.

"I guess I wouldn't mind a glass of red if you have it."

NINE

ELIZABETH

THE GLASS OF SHIRAZ I practically inhaled at the house did absolutely nothing to quash my nerves. The muscles in my neck and shoulders tense up the moment I step into the restaurant. The delectable scents of meat, garlic, and a hot grill are wafting through the air, making my stomach rumble, and I can hear raucous laughter coming from the back. I'm entering the private room of the upscale Albright Bar & Steakhouse. The place where twenty-five family members I've never met are celebrating my uncle's birthday.

"Nervous?" My aunt asks while gently rubbing my back.

"A little," I admit. Kind of wishing she would stop touching me. It's only making me more rattled.

That and the fact that I'm completely underdressed like I feared I would be. It is crystal clear upon first glance that the people in this room have spent what my app made over the last two months on their outfits. I should have realized what I was dealing with when I took a first look at Juliette's outfit.

She is wearing a cream-colored pair of Armani slacks and a cream boat-necked silk shell, both of which seem to skim the length of her body. Not too tight, not too baggy, and both make her look like a million bucks. Her hair is pulled back in an elegantly smooth ponytail, and she has expertly applied colors from a nude make up palette, which make her glow and her entire outfit look even more polished. Nude leather stilettos finish the ensemble.

I on the other hand am wearing a pair of tight, white skinny jeans, my "dressy" white scoop neck t-shirt, and the only pair of nice wedge sandals I own. All from Target (pronounced Tarjay with an accent, thank you very much). The complete outfit probably set me back about fifty bucks, and it's very basic, but it's also probably the most flattering outfit I own. You don't dress up much when you're on the computer all day and night and you're broke. My wardrobe consists mostly of T-shirts and yoga pants.

I've never really known what to do with my massive head of curly hair. I have repeatedly failed at mastering the art of blowing it out or flat ironing it properly. My mother told me the key to a perfect coif was to use the right products, but she offered very little information on what those right products might be for me. Typical of my mom. Direction without substance. So I pull it back in a semi-messy ponytail, like I do most days, and hope no one will think that I didn't at least try.

When I enter the room with Juliette, I immediately hesitate because all eyes focus in my direction and they grow eerily quiet. I'm sure some silence is because Juliette has the distinct ability to command attention when she walks into a room, besides the fact that I'm the new girl in the family.

"Everyone, this is Elizabeth. Elizabeth, this is everyone."

I can hear the joy in my aunt's voice when she introduces me. She's genuinely happy that I'm here, and there's definitely something about her exuberance which saddens me, because I totally feel like I'm using her. I can see my mother's, "I told you so" face in my head right now. I should have reached out to my aunt way before I needed something from her. I've lived in this same city for over five years. Whatever her issues are with my father has nothing to do with me.

A somewhat familiar looking, handsome older man, dressed in a crisp white shirt and metal gray suit steps forward. He has a head full of deep wavy dark hair, with a little salt and pepper at the temples that I can tell he must tame using a lot of products. His face is serious, but his eyes are wildly expressive with lines that crinkle in the corners. He exudes pure confidence and dominance in the room without appearing arrogant. I deduce that this man must be Juliette's husband. The infamous Uncle Joseph.

"Hi, Elizabeth. I'm Joseph."

The room is deadly silent now. I'm unsure of why. I feel like I'm in the middle of a Godfather movie.

I smile awkwardly. "Happy Birthday, Uncle Joseph."

I extend my hand to shake his, but he moves forward, bypassing my extended hand, and slowly embraces me. I can feel some tension in his body, but I'm not really clear why it's there. Maybe because this is sort of awkward for the both of us.

"Just call me Joseph." I nod in agreement.

"I look forward to getting to know you." "Me too," I say.

I hear some light chatter in the room begin again and when my uncle releases me; he turns to slowly and lovingly embrace my aunt.

"Thank you for this," he says to her. Gliding a few of his

knuckles down the side of her face. Staring into her eyes like she's the only woman in the room.

"Happy Birthday, Honey." She softly says, almost with a blush to her cheeks.

I'm not going to lie. I'm surprised by their intense affection for each other. They look like they are very much in love. I'm not sure what I was expecting, but this wasn't it. My parents don't look at each other this way, and neither do my friends' parents. It's kind of nice.

As the evening continues, I meet several more of my relatives in the room and am amazed that each person seems nicer than the next. I'm tired, though. Physically and mentally. It's exhausting faking a smile and conducting idle chitchat with people you don't know. One after the other.

I decide to excuse myself from the main room and find a restroom to give myself a break. After I pee, wash my hands, and finish talking myself into returning to the party, I take the long way back to the party room and pass through a seating area where people are waiting for tables in the main dining room. I notice an unoccupied seat, so I sit down for a second and text Sloan. Anything to buy me a few more minutes away from my well-intentioned but smothering new family.

Before I know it, some snot-nosed tween with freckles and a mischievous look on his face races me for the seat. He swiftly brushes behind me and plops his butt in my spot. I can imagine the look on his mother's face if I end up ass first in this kid's lap, but it's hard for me to stop my backward momentum. My ankle turns (thank you very much wedge sandals), and now I'm falling. I turn my body just enough, so that I'll hopefully end up on the floor and not on top of freckle face. Although I'm betting, he wouldn't mind.

"Down goes Frazier!" The kid says gleefully as I fall right on my butt.

While I'm totally embarrassed, and paranoid because I'm wearing white and have zero idea what nastiness could be on this floor, I'm impressed that this little deviant even knows who Joe Frazier was. I'm twice this kid's age, and the only reason I know the heavyweight fighter's name is because he's a Philadelphia legend and fought Muhammad Ali.

Before I can help myself up, all my spidey senses raise to a high alert.

I feel him before I can even see him.

"You all right?" A heavy voice asks me with a look of concern, but also laced with a sprinkling of what I think is laughter in his voice. I nod my head up and down like a speechless idiot while the voice pulls me up to my feet and balances me around my waist.

It's him ... in all his badass, muscular, one-dimpled splendor.

What I'm feeling right now is hard to explain. My stomach is swirling inside due to a weird brew of excitement and fear. What are the chances of me running into the same guy in this restaurant, when I'm flat on my ass ... again? Actually, scratch that. It explains everything. I have the worst luck.

"Yes, thanks," I finally say.

He begins to methodically brush my ass and the backs of my thighs off, using slow broad strokes with the palm of his hand, and I'm embarrassed to admit to myself just how good it feels to have his hands on me. Especially there.

"Just getting off the dirt," he assures me with a wink. He then turns to freckle face with a stern look on his face.

"You should always give up your seat to a lady. Didn't anyone ever teach you that, kid?"

The boy's face drops.

"Yeah."

"Yes, what?"

"Yes, sir," he answers petulantly.

The stranger nods his head and turns back to face me. He's still holding me loosely around the waist, mind you, and I have yet to make any attempt to move from under his protection.

"Can I buy you a drink?" he asks.

"Umm–"

"You having dinner with someone?" His face looks tight.

"A private party."

"So you don't have to get back right away then?"

"Well–"

"What do you drink?"

Just like outside Club Lotus, every woman in the waiting area and adjoining bar seems to gaze at the stranger. Drooling over him. It's actually quite interesting to watch. I did not understand that women really acted like this. It's ridiculous. I mean, I've gawked at a few men over the course of my travels too, but nothing as overt as how they are ogling his entire body. Flipping their hair. Licking their lips. He must be used to it though, because he barely seems to notice or care at the moment. I'm sure he can get a woman into his bed at any given time. No need to concern himself with it now.

"Red wine is fine," I say.

I wonder if he's surprised. Women my age rarely opt for wine. Most of my friends would have ordered shots or something fruity and frozen, but I grew up sneaking sips of my mom's nightly glass of cabernet, so it is familiar to me. Something I know I can order and enjoy.

Plus, I've always thought that wine was a very classy drink to order.

I watch carefully as the stranger grabs us a high top table with two stools. I don't like how awkwardly I'm carrying myself. Like the new kid at the lunch table looking for the right words to say. I bravely look up into his eyes, thinking maybe the words will come, but now I wish I hadn't.

"What's wrong?" He asks gently.

"What–"

"You're in pain." He observes.

I clamp my mouth shut. My wrist was hurting a little from trying to break my fall. Plus, I'm not sure that I'm totally healed from the attack. Sometimes I wake up with aches in weird places. I must have fallen harder than I thought to the ground when I was punched in the jaw.

He pauses for a moment, then grasps my arm. "Did you hurt yourself when you fell?"

I flinch slightly when he handles my arm. Not so much from the pain, but because I'm still skittish. When he notices my reaction, he abruptly stands and strides over to the bar to grab the bartender's attention.

"One second, Elizabeth."

The bartender is a tall bleached blonde wearing a tight black t-shirt and leggings. Her face isn't overtly pretty, but I can see how men would consider her attractive. She immediately flirts with my stranger, as he appears to be placing a drink order. At least I think that's what he's doing. They're doing a lot of damn talking for just a simple drink order.

I think what irritates me the most, is that it almost seems effortless between them. The conversation. The smiles. Her hair flipping. Her chest lifted high and forward with confidence. I have limited experience with guys; I wouldn't know how to flirt with a guy if my life depended on it. Not like she's doing. It's actually pretty sad.

The flirty bartender leans over the counter and whispers something in the stranger's ear, and he immediately looks back at me. I wonder what she's saying? Embarrassed that I'm gawking at the two of them, I swiftly bow my head and start fiddling with my phone. Not smooth at all. I know that I've been caught like a kid digging up her nose. That's why I'm startled, but a little relieved when my phone actually buzzes to life. It's a legitimate distraction. It's a text from Sloan.

Sloan: Hey, hooker!

Me: Hey

Sloan: What's up?

Me: You will not believe this.

Sloan: What!!?

Me: I'm out with the family at a restaurant and HE'S here.

Sloan: Who?

Me: The stranger from the club.

Sloan: Oh. My. God. Is he fucking stalking you:)

Me: Did you type a smiley face bc I have a stalker?

A strange, prickly sensation flutters across the back of my neck.

Damn, he's back already.

Me: I gotta go

Sloan: Wait, we didn't–

I quickly put my phone to sleep, because he's definitely back and standing close behind me with two glasses in his hands, along with a man in an ill-fitting oxford shirt and khakis standing next to him.

"I was just finishing a text to a friend," I explain like the bumbling idiot I am. As if he cares.

"I see that." He sits in the chair on the left side of me and hands me a glass of wine. "This is Mr. Edmonds. He's the manager of this fine establishment." He exaggerates the word fine as if it's anything but.

"I heard you had a slight accident in the waiting area, Miss–"

"Elizabeth."

I take a sip then set my glass down.

"Elizabeth, on behalf of management, I'd like to extend my deepest apologies. It's our fault that the area was so crowded. We have to do a better job of managing walk-ins and getting folks seated faster."

I dip my head in agreement, but I honestly don't really believe this is the restaurant's fault. I fell down completely on my own, but I can tell by the manager's bleak face, that he wants me to accept whatever he has prepared to say, so he can get on with the rest of his night. He seems nervous. Perhaps because the stranger is giving him a steely look that would scare the hell out of just about anyone. So I just let poor Mr. Edmonds continue on with his totally unnecessary spiel.

"As a courtesy, I'd like to cover your drinks for tonight and add a credit to your party's bill."

Oh crap! The party. How long have I been gone?

"Well, that's very kind of you, Mr. Edmonds. But it was totally my–"

"You may want to speak to that kid's parents," the stranger abruptly interrupts. "They were nowhere in the vicinity when this whole thing happened. I'm concerned for you as well with liability issues and all."

"Of course, sir." He turns to me, "I actually remember the party you came in with, Miss. I'll be sure to credit the check appropriately."

Mr. Edmonds fidgets with his watch and waits for what I think is his dismissal. The stranger just stares at him, waiting. It's an uneasy standoff. I can tell that the stranger takes great pleasure in punking other men. Not something I approve of, but I admit it's nice to know that he can handle himself. As if there was ever any doubt.

"Ok well ... you both have a pleasant evening and enjoy your meal."

The stranger nods with a smug look on his face.

I smile at Mr. Edmonds, and hope that he realizes that my grin is not a self-satisfied one but more of an apology than anything.

"You could have let me finish what I was going to say to the poor man," I say to the stranger as soon as Mr. Edmonds walks away.

"I could have, but it sounded like you were going to say that it was totally your fault or some such bullshit."

I suck in a breath of surprise at his bluntness. "Well, it was my fault."

"Nope," he says matter-of-factly. "It wasn't."

"Well, thank you anyhow."

"No thanks necessary, but I would like something in return."

"What?" I ask, shifting my feet nervously.

"Relax, Duchess. I just want you to stay and finish your drink with me."

"Duchess? Umm–" I squirm a little, not knowing how to respond to being given a nickname by him. I like it, but I damn sure don't want to like it.

"We're not strangers anymore." He flashes a delicious grin featuring that dimple of his again, and I could just melt on the spot. "And I give all my friends nicknames."

I watch him swirl and sip on what looks and smells like a whiskey highball. His posture exuding nothing but sheer dominance. Tonight he's wearing a pair of black pants with a black button-down shirt, sleeves loosely rolled up mid-forearm, and a pair of black chucks to dress it all down. His five o'clock shadow is heavier today and like someone with a zit on their face, my eyes seem to be constantly drawn to the scar on his face.

He's so frackin' beautiful, I can't stand it.

As I gawk at him, he seems to be quietly studying me as well. Like he's trying to figure me out, as if I'm some sort of brain-teaser or five thousand piece jigsaw puzzle. There's something about the way he observes me which is extremely unnerving and provocative.

"Why are you looking at me like that?" I blurt out before I even realize what I'm saying.

"How am I looking at you?"

"Like a piece of chicken."

Someone tape my mouth shut, please.

He lets out a low chuckle, highlighting that lone dimple again, which gives me the sudden urge to crawl up his body like a flagpole and lick the side of his face. I wish. "I'm not a big talker, so I prefer to observe."

"Then why did you want me to have a drink with you? To just observe me?" I giggle nervously.

He moves closer to me. "Do you have a man, Duchess?"

I look down at my feet when I answer his question. "Absolutely not."

"Oh, absolutely not. That's a strong statement. Not looking for anything serious, are we?" He lifts my chin with his fingers.

"Nope, I'm not looking for anything serious or casual." I hesitantly look in his eyes to gauge his reaction to my comment.

"Staying away from all men then?"

"Yep, they haven't been so good for my health." I try to joke when in actuality I'm serious as all hell.

He leans his head to the side. "So, the fact that I have zero chance is what you're so eloquently trying to say."

I stare at him, stunned. It was plain as day that he could have any woman he wanted, but was he actually saying he had some sort of actual interest in me?

"I guess that's what I'm saying."

I'm not even sure I believe the words coming out of my mouth.

"Bad relationship?"

"Something like that."

He pauses a moment and his body language shifts before he says the next thing.

"Have you ever had a no-strings sexual relationship with a man, Duchess?"

I choke a little on my wine. He wants to have sex with me? That would be lovely if I wasn't such a scaredy-cat. There's no way in hell an inexperienced mess like me is going to sleep with someone like him. That's why I decide that I need to immediately shut this conversation down and get back to my party, before I say anything stupid like, no, but I want one with you.

"Umm no, but listen, thanks so much for your help yet

again, but I have to get back to my party. They're probably worried. Maybe I'll see you around."

And I ran out of there like a bat out of hell, before he could stop me.

Even though a small part of me totally wished that he would have tried.

TEN

ROMAN

I SHOULD HAVE STOPPED HER from running.

That's what a smart man would have done. Damn, she was beautiful. Those white jeans hugging every one of her mouth-watering curves like a glove. Those perfect tits. That fucking mouth. Those eyes, almond-shaped and evocative. I'd love to know what she was thinking about that made her eyes wary of me for just a moment, then warm, then something else. It's the something else that I'm most interested in. I'm not used to that type of layered reaction from a woman. I'm used to attraction and definitely lust, but not whatever that was.

I'm not a superstitious person, but there's no way in hell that I can't recognize a sign when I see one. I see this woman twice in a week and both times I find her on the ground needing my help. I made my mind up to start looking for her at The Lotus and not even twenty-four hours later; she appears to me like a water apparition to a thirsty man in the hot desert. At the very least, I need to know who she is, why she keeps ending up in the middle of the floor, and why the fuck she keeps running from me. I figure the easiest path to the information I need may be obtained if I head back over to the chatty blond bartender.

"I'm looking for Edmonds," I say to her.

"What do you need with him again?" she asks seductively. "Maybe I can help you."

She whips all of her hair to the side, so that I have a clearer view of the side of her slender neck and her breasts. She has a nice rack, but she's not who or what I'm interested in at the moment.

"The woman I was talking to. I need to know which private party she's with."

"Why?" she asks with a tinge of jealousy in her voice. I'm used to women being territorial with me, and typically I enjoy it, but I don't have the patience for this shit right now.

"Do you know or not?"

Her mouth twists in disapproval, but she gives me an answer, anyway.

"She's in the Madison room."

"Madison?" I repeat.

"Yep," she answers dismissively as she goes to take an order from another patron.

That's the room my party is in.

Joseph's party.

The only other sign I need.

She's mine.

WHEN I ENTER THE DOORS OF The Madison room,
I immediately start scanning the room looking for Elizabeth, but unfortunately lock eyes with the old man first. I can see the disapproval simmering behind the frozen glare he's giving me. It's his birthday, and his precious Juliette

threw him a party for which I am late. He's not going to say anything to me about it, but he doesn't have to. The look he's throwing my way says it all. My father has always been tough on me. I'm used to it. So I nod to him in acknowledgement of his birthday and in silent apology for being late as well. I'm sure he'll make me pay for it in some other way in the very near future.

When I was a kid and my mother took off for over three weeks, which was the longest stretch of time she had ever left home, I ran out of food and money and finally broke down and called Joseph. We weren't close like a typical father and son, but I was desperate. I didn't know it at the time, but my mother was suffering from bipolar disorder in addition to being an addict. She would sometimes leave to go on a binge but had never been missing that long. When Joseph came to pick me up he told me, "You're never coming back here again. So make your peace with it. You're going to be better than this. Forget about this place."

For a while, things were good. I tried to be the son that Joseph wanted me to be. Smart. Respectful. Appreciative. Controlled. Ambitious. The son of a rising millionaire. But I'd been taking care of my mother and myself a little too long in the 'hood to let go of all of my bad habits. My dirty mouth. My temper. My trust issues. My problem-solving skills. My penchant for pussy.

As I grew older and started working for Joseph, my bad habits seemed to mushroom, and the distance between us grew even wider. Things came to a head when he politely announced that I had exactly seven days to find another place to live. I remember it exactly, because it was also the same day I came frighteningly close to killing a man. My knuckles were purple, bruised, swollen, and my fingernails still carried traces of the man's crusty dried blood underneath them. I hadn't hurt this particular man because he threatened my life or did something to seriously piss me off.

I did it strictly because Joseph asked me to handle a work issue, which I allowed to get completely out of hand. While I definitely had given out my fair share of beat downs in the past, kicking someone's ass beyond the point of reasonable was an entirely different thing for me. Especially because I almost beat this guy to the brink of death.

The man's name was Carl. I'll always remember that name. Anytime I hear it, my eye inadvertently twitches. He was in the ICU for five days, and they had to resuscitate him twice. Luckily for me, Joseph took care of the details, and I was never a formal suspect in the beating, even though there was DNA evidence all over the place. The police filed it as an unsolved gang-related assault, thanks to a few connections my father had at the precinct. Although I faced no charges for it, there was something about almost beating a man to death that stuck with me.

It changed me.

And the change has been darkening, growing, and curling inside me ever since.

That's what my father sees when he looks at me - darkness, disappointment, lack of control.

Joseph comes from the very same humble beginnings that I do, and in order for him to carve out the immense success that he has, I understand that he's had to make tough decisions. Sacrifices. Choices that have cost him a lot. When you make those sorts of choices in life, there are always consequences, and he never likes to look back. I think I remind him of what's back there. What he comes from. What he's had to do. What he now looks upon with disdain and would like to forget. He's rather fucking hypocritical though, and sometimes I'd really like to tell him how much of a hypocrite he is.

Joseph started out his career doing exactly what I do.

As a fixer.

A man that other men hire to make their problems go away by any means necessary. He worked in the mailroom of a law firm where a then young and upcoming lawyer named Jack Mills hired him to make a paternity suit go away for one of his clients. No experience required. Jack thought he saw something in Joseph's eyes that told him that the problem would be handled. And it was. Joseph never talks about the details of how he handled that case, but rumor has it that he beat the crap out of the woman's younger brother until she agreed to recant her statement and drop the paternity case for a ridiculously low settlement. Something disrespectful, like a settlement for a thousand dollars. It was the best beating Joseph ever gave, in my opinion. It changed his life and mine in the best way possible. Sometimes I think he forgets that.

With the increased popularity of the Internet, cell phone use, and social media, it was easier than ever for the public to find out all about the trouble celebrities were getting into. This was great for Joseph's new consultant business, because he was gaining the reputation of being one of the best in the business. When it became glaringly obvious during my high school years that I inherited Joseph's natural tendency to fuck somebody up with little remorse, I then became his protégé. His heir apparent. Or more accurately put his muscle.

I do the shit that he no longer wants to do. The dirty stuff. The rough shit. But the reason why Joseph is still one of the most highly sought after fixers on the East Coast is because of his ability to handle problems swiftly, quietly and without loose ends. The Carl incident almost fucked up his pristine reputation, and Joseph never forgets mistakes, especially when he's not the one making the mistake.

Carl was a two-bit dealer who was selling weed to a very popular teenaged Disney star, who he later black-mailed when the kid started using another dealer. I didn't understand why he was resorting to blackmail over one lost customer, but it wasn't my job to understand why idiots do what they do. It was my job to get him to see reason very damn quickly. Joseph's kind of reason.

Unfortunately, just when I thought Carl, and I were coming to an understanding, he spat in my face. Something I don't take kindly to. So I pummeled him ... again. And just when I thought to myself for a split second that it wasn't my fight, that I should walk away and have Joseph find some-body else to deal with him, he mustered up the strength and the balls to tell me to "Go fuck yourself, you piece of trash."

And that was it.

Something snapped inside of my brain. Something old and festered, that I preferred to keep locked away deep inside of me, rose up front and center. And that's when I kicked Carl's ass one last and final time, until I made sure that he couldn't say one more fucking thing out of his swollen, bloody mouth.

During that final beating, my heart was racing as my fists hit the side of his skull, my breathing was heavy as I cracked and kicked in the sides of his ribs, and my nostrils were flaring like a wild animal's as I paced and circled around his limp body waiting for him to make a move.

I felt alive and powerful, as if it was an out-of-body experience. There was a definite high I felt when I was in the middle of a fight, but this was different. He'd called me trash, and like I said, something snapped. I wasn't trying to fight him; I was trying to finish him.

Yet when I was done, and my breathing slowed, and I took a really long look at the man lying stock still in a pool of his own blood, I didn't feel justified or powerful or alive anymore. I was scared. Scared that I had killed the little fucker, and that I had enough blind rage inside of me to actually have done something like that.

It hadn't been a fair fight. It hadn't been a fight at all. So I just felt like shit. Dirty. Like there was a layer of grime that no matter how much I wanted to, I just couldn't seem to get rid of. Like there was something really wrong with me that everyone could see. That my father could probably see.

Joseph fined me for my Carl fuck up. Three thousand dollars, which was a hell of a lot of money for me back then. He said I needed to cover the costs of all the people he needed to pay off to make sure this stayed out of the news and off any do-gooder police detective's radar. He explained that normally it would have been five thousand dollars, but that I'd need the extra two grand to move out of his house in the next seven days.

Joseph also lectured me. Every day for three days. He wanted to make it very much clear that this was a business he built from the ground up, and that he wasn't going to let his "off-the-rails bastard son ruin everything that he'd worked so hard for."

He emphasized that control was the key ingredient to his success, and that I needed to stay focused and show no signs of weakness ever again. He told me that he never wanted the ugliness of what we were sometimes forced to do in our work to ever show up on his doorstep. To dirty his clean life. His clean life with Juliette. And because I couldn't totally be trusted to keep those things separate and apart, I'd need to live somewhere else.

I HEAR THE SWEETEST LAUGH that I've ever heard.

The laughter of an angel.

It's floating above the murmur of all the voices in the room, distracting me from my father's disapproval, and I know instantaneously that it's her. I also know that if it's a man making her laugh like that, that I'm going to politely drag his ass out of Joseph's party and kick his ass until he begs for his mommy.

My father was right.

I sure as hell can't be trusted.

ELEVEN

ELIZABETH

THE MADISON ROOM IN THE Albright Bar & Steakhouse has a tiny makeshift dance floor, which is kind of weird, because it's such an upscale place. One would think they could do better. In fact, the dance area looks like it comprises only about fifteen linoleum tiles, definitely not up to the standards of the rest of the restaurant, but it's clear that my family is going to do their damnedest to make it a party. I must admit, I kind of like them for that.

Everyone in here is practically rich, but they're still a lot of fun. Not stiff like most of the people I know back home, who are barely making their mortgages but act a hell of a lot snootier.

Juliette must have weaved some of her party magic and persuaded the restaurant to pipe in one of her special playlists through the room's speaker system. I'm pretty sure it's the same playlist she was exercising to earlier. It's full of old radio hits. Most I recognize thanks to my mom, but a few I don't.

I'm laughing heartily at a thin woman with a silver-gray bob and a tasteful blue floral dress on named Aunt Joan, who is telling me a funny story about each person who gets up to dance. Aunt Joan must be tipsy, because she is sipping on something called an Old Fashion and telling the same stories twice, but they're funny nonetheless.

Then I feel the prickle again.

I rub the back of my neck gently with my fingertips.

It can't be. It can't frackin' be.

"Hello again, Duchess."

I raise my head and meet a set of coal-black eyes that are pinning me to my seat.

"Hi," is all I manage to squeak out.

He continues to stand there, gazing at my mouth, while Aunt Joan looks between the two of us like she's watching a tennis match. Heat is emanating off the back of my neck, and I'm breaking into a slight sweat. You'd have to be an idiot not to notice how he is affecting me, and Aunt Joan seems like she's far from being anyone's idiot.

Did he follow me or did he actually come looking for me? I know that I should be frightened by his stalkerish tendencies, but instead I'm gushing wet because of it.

"Let's dance," he says in a thick voice.

It's not a question or a request, but more like this is what we're going to do now. I can't refuse. My body won't allow it.

"All right."

There's a weird mid-tempo song playing, which makes me wonder how we're going to dance with each other. It's not slow enough for a slow dance, and it's not fast enough to dance apart normally. The decision is taken out of my hands when he gently pulls me into his arms and starts to gently rock back and forth to the beat of the song.

One of his massive legs slides in between my two quivering ones, and his moves are smooth and strong enough that he rocks my body along with his, which only encourages other much more x-rated thoughts to pop into my head. Especially when I feel something rock solid poking me in my abdomen.

"What are you thinking about right this second?" he lowers his head to whisper in my ear.

Your intoxicating smell.

How hard you are.

"Popcorn," I blurt out. Really, Elizabeth?

"Popcorn?"

"It's my favorite snack."

I'm a bumbling embarrassment to every woman on the planet right now.

"You're hungry right now?" he asks incredulously.

I giggle, "A little."

"No one fed you in here?" He chuckles when he asks me that.

"I missed most of dinner when I was having a glass of merlot with a certain stranger earlier."

"Then I owe you dinner." He smiles. "When do you want to collect?"

I can't help but blush from his forwardness, especially when he pulls me closer to him. I smell whiskey, chocolate, and an additional scent that is completely unique to him.

He could bottle that shit up and sell it.

Stay focused, Elizabeth.

"I don't have dinner with strangers."

I say no to dinner, because let's be realistic here. What on earth does he want with me? And what on earth would I do with him? I'm a basket case. A mess.

And he's, not.

"You think we're still strangers? Ok, let's fix that

problem right now. Tell me five things about yourself." He points his finger at me and orders, "Go."

"Five things? That's not going to really change things."

"It'll change everything," he says resolutely.

Everything he says is frackin' sexy.

Both of his hands slip lower to the base of my spine. He hooks his thumbs into the belt loops of my jeans and lets his hands loosely lay on the top of my ass as we continue to rock to the song that's playing.

Everything he does is frackin' sexy.

"I love popcorn–" I say breathlessly, forgetting that I've already mentioned that.

"I already know that. Five other things," he urges.

I start rattling off stats like a complete moron.

"My favorite color is yellow. I love dogs, not cats. I graduated in the top ten percent of my high school class. I'm an only child, and I don't really know anyone here tonight."

"You crashed the party?" He smirks with approval.

"I didn't say that exactly–"

"Where are you from?" he interrupts.

"Uh-uh. I gave you my five things. It's your turn."

I'm not sure where that burst of confidence came from, but it's probably the most Bitsy-like thing I've said in his presence since we've met. Finally! I was a leader in high school, a force to be reckoned with in college, and now I'm a budding entrepreneur. I'm not some mealy mouthed virgin who melts at the sight of every badass who crosses my path.

I think I hear him growl in protest at the base of his throat. I'm not so sure that he likes how I threw things back into his court, but I'm not going to budge. I'll just quietly keep dancing with him until he answers me.

"All right. My favorite color is blue. I own an Alaskan

Malamute named Mr. Tibbs. I hated high school, and I'm an only child too."

"That's only four," I point out.

He doesn't reply, but instead rubs a few strands of my curly ponytail between his fingers, and I attempt to hide the smile that's widening across my face against his chest. Ok, maybe I am acting like a mealy mouthed virgin.

"Mr. Tibbs?" I ask to break the trance that his stroking of my hair is placing me in.

"He has crystal blue eyes the color of the Caribbean Sea, and he's mean as shit. You'll see when you meet him."

When I meet him? I smile very brightly to myself because I like the words, even though I know he only wants to get in between my legs. He made that quite clear earlier.

Our song ends, but another mid-tempo song I've heard on the radio about ten years ago begins.

"Old people and their music," he snickers. "I hate this crap."

"We can sit down if you want," I offer.

Maybe he's sick of dancing with me, but he keeps his grip firmly around my center, while we keep rocking back and forth to the rhythm of the song. I'm beginning to really like how I feel inside his embrace. His one leg wedged in between my two. My head tucked underneath his chin. How close I am to all his hard edges.

"I'd really like for us not to be strangers," he says in a gravelly voice that I could very well become addicted to. "Did my five things work?"

"Four things—" I correct him. "And no, they didn't work. I've met you twice, you've told me four random things about yourself, but you forgot the most important."

"What's that?"

"Your name. Remember, I don't eat with strangers or talk to strangers." I grin.

"Well, what will you do with strangers?" he asks with a glint in his hard, obsidian eyes.

"Nothing," I say, as if it's the hardest thing I've ever admitted to in my life.

"I'd like to change your mind about that, Elizabeth."

"I don't think so." But I want him so badly that my mouth is practically salivating.

I notice several pairs of eyes on us as we dance, but think little of it, because the stranger's lips are directly above my ear now, causing me to block out any further distractions.

"This stranger is seriously considering bending you over one of these round tables in front of all the rest of these people, and giving you the privilege of calling me whatever name you choose, while I make you come hard with my fingers, then my tongue, then my cock."

What. The. Frack.

I wasn't expecting him to say anything remotely close to that, and so my legs almost buckle from underneath me from the images he's so eloquently described in fantastically dirty detail. He deserves a slap for that, but before I can pretend that I'm insulted by his overtly sexual comments, we're suddenly interrupted by the hilarious aunt I was chatting with earlier. I'm not sure if I'm relieved or annoyed by her interruption.

"I see you two have already reconnected," she says with a small, dubious grin on her face.

"Reconnected?" I ask, unclear by what she means.

"Juliette!" she calls across the room. "Come here, honey. I believe you have some introductions to make."

The stranger stops dancing and pulls away from me when he sees Juliette approach.

I miss the warmth of his body already.

"Oh, I see you're finally here," Juliette says to him.

Wait, my aunt knows Mr. Badass?

"Hey," he says while giving her a hug and a brief kiss on the side of her face.

"Hi yourself, stranger. Did you two recognize each other?"

"Why would we?" he asks, looking back over at me.

A sick feeling grows in the pit of my belly.

"Oh well, I guess you wouldn't," she chuckles. "You've only seen each other once when you were kids, so let me do the honors. Elizabeth, this is Roman Masterson—my stepson. Roman, this is your cousin Elizabeth. My brother Patrick's daughter."

I swallow what feels like the largest lump of dry cotton down my throat. I didn't recognize the face, but I definitely remember the name.

"You're Roman!" I didn't mean to say that as loudly as I did, but I'm completely mortified.

I squeeze my eyes shut for a moment in utter embarrassment at what almost transpired between the two of us. When my eyes rise to meet Roman's, I can't help but wonder what he's thinking right now, but I can't read him. Not until he speaks to me in a tone that makes my hackles rise.

"Nice to see you again, little sunflower," he says in an almost delighted tone.

And I'm pretty sure that I just threw up a little in my mouth.

TWELVE

ROMAN

I AM TRYING TO SPEND AS little time at my father's house as humanly possible. This is the second week in a row that I've stayed busy either working, drinking, or fucking random women. I'm not sure how much longer I can keep this going, not when I promised Joseph that I'd handle whatever trouble my little cousin was in.

Of course, I assured him of all of this way before I spotted her in the middle of the Club Lotus dance floor. Completely before, I fantasized about claiming all of her orgasms for the next year. Totally before I propositioned her at my father's birthday party. Absolutely before I learned that she is my fucking cousin.

I've thought about running by the house a million times. Even though I don't live there anymore, I still have a room there. Juliette insisted on it and didn't care what Joseph had to say about it. And even though we have an office on South Broad, Joseph likes to handle a lot of his business out of their home. He's old school. He likes to fax versus email, the phone over texting, and he absolutely prefers talking in person above all of that. I think it's because he likes to look you in the eyes and see if you're lying or not. So, he's always asking me to swing by the house to talk to me about this or pick up that. I should have been by the house a million times by now.

But I can't do it.

Why? Because when I'm near Elizabeth, I have this unexplainable craving to touch her. Now that I've held her in my arms once, I can't help but want to hold her again. Preferably in a horizontal position. It's pretty pathetic how I regress into a horny thirteen-year-old boy when I think about Elizabeth. I haven't seen her since the night of Joseph's party, but my dick has been brick hard fantasizing about her every single fucking day since.

Totally wound up last night from all my pent up frustration, I couldn't sleep and found myself thinking about her. Imagining if I stayed over the house and pulled Elizabeth into my old bedroom. I'd sit her on the edge of my bed, dressed in only a thong and a pair of heels by my special request. I don't even know if she wears thongs, but hey it's my fantasy. She'd spread her legs on my command, and then I'd get on my knees, slide her thong over slowly and lick her clit expertly and thoroughly until she cried for release.

Fuck.

I don't even want to say out loud to myself how fucked up this is, because blood or no blood, Elizabeth is family. She is Juliette's niece, and I respect Juliette. She's been nothing but good to me ever since I was a kid, which means I need to treat her niece like a cousin; not like my next piece of ass.

The old man is no fool either. If I keep avoiding the house for too much longer, he's going to know something is up. He's paid well to know shit before other people do. To sense shit. If he really starts paying any serious attention to my behavior around Elizabeth, or rather my inability to be around Elizabeth, he will immediately see right through me, and he won't like it.

The only thing keeping the nosy bastard off my case is the fact that he's preoccupied with the Mendez job. A baseball steroids case. It pays a shitload of money if we can get to any potential witnesses and pay them to say exactly what we want them to say during his hearing with Major League Baseball. Joseph hasn't asked for my help on it yet, which is fine by me. I've got my hands full with a million other things.

In my lame effort to avoid all things Elizabeth this week, I slept with a bank manager named Louise. What a head case. She's been full-blown phone stalking me for the last twenty-four hours, and I have no one to blame but myself. I have always forgotten the last woman with the next, but this time the shit isn't working. Instead, all I've created for myself is a colossal headache. So rather than getting some meaningless head tonight from another crazy woman, I've decided to drink myself senseless with the fun snatcher—Camden. Getting trashed with someone more miserable than me is a lot simpler than trolling for pussy.

"Pass me an egg roll."

"Take all of them. I don't want to eat any more of this shit," I gripe.

"Are you on your period? You are acting like a real bitch."

"And you aren't?"

Camden has been my friend for over ten years. We met our junior year of high school when we got into a fight in gym class over a girl named Samantha Minta. Pretty smile and a fat ass, but not worth the week's detention we both received for fighting on school property. We've been cool ever since.

"I have to keep an eye on my cousin, and I don't feel like it," I lamely explain.

"That's why you're so pissy? Fuck it, I'll do it. Is she hot?"

Just the question alone made me want to kick Camden straight in the teeth. It wasn't his fault, though. I haven't told him anything about Elizabeth. He has no idea that I'm lusting after my own damn cousin, but there's no way in hell that I'd tell him. I mean, if he told me something like that, I'd probably beat his ass just because.

"Drop it, Cam."

"Why? Is she a wildebeast?"

"You've been watching National Geographic again?" I smirk.

"What's wrong with her, asshole?"

"Nothing's *wrong* with her."

"Protective, are we then?"

"Not really," I try to say nonchalantly. "I just don't want you trying to fuck her. She's family."

"Why don't you just send Jade over there then? Make her take her out or something."

"It's more complicated than taking her out. She's in some sort of trouble. Joseph wants me to handle it."

"Well, that's even easier then. It's a babysitting job with a purpose."

By purpose, I bet he doesn't mean me plotting and planning on how many ways I'm going to make Elizabeth call out my name in agonizing bliss.

"Yeah, I guess," I mutter.

Camden squirts a little duck sauce on his egg roll and takes a bite.

"So what does Joseph plan on doing with the club?"

"I don't know. I just know he's tasked me with the job of whipping the motherfucker back into shape, after we planned its self destruction so perfectly."

"That's what we do," Camden says somewhat sarcastically. "We've done it a hundred times. We did it with that club on Second Street and we're going to have to do it with The Lotus. What else is new? I just wish I knew what he wants with a couple of local night spots. He probably will make triple what those clubs would make in a year just by handling the Mendez job. It makes no sense."

I can hear the doubt in Camden's voice. I'm not judging. He's probably right to question Joseph's motives. I just need to know where my friend's head is at. I don't need any Joseph/Camden shit blowing up in my face.

"What the hell is your real problem with the old man? What aren't you telling me?"

"Nothing, man. Just talking out loud," he brushes the topic off. "So this cousin of yours, she's over twenty-one right?"

"Yeah, I'm pretty sure Juliette mentioned that she was twenty-three or four."

I'm such a fucking joke right now. Juliette didn't tell me shit, because she didn't have to. I already know my cousin's age and just about every other thing that's on public record for one Miss Elizabeth Hill from Penn-Washington, Pennsylvania.

She's never had a parking ticket, she has zero student loans, but she's up to her eyeballs in credit card debt. She has a few social media accounts that she isn't really active on unless she's talking about college debt or some gibberish. She also has a rather large medical bill on record, seeing as though she was hospitalized recently for a head concussion and minor lacerations. An incident I won't tell Joseph anything about until I know more.

"So what's she doing living with them?"

"I'm assuming it has something to do with the trouble she's in, idiot. Did you not hear anything I said? All I know is she lost her apartment or something. She used to live over by the art museum. It's my job to find out why."

"You want me to run a check?"

At Masterson & Associates, I am the muscle, Cutter is the schmoozer, and Camden is the techie. He spent a lot of our youth breaking into computer systems for fun, and now he gets paid by Joseph to do it. Usually to gain leverage over someone. He might be able to find out everything I need to know about Elizabeth with a few simple strokes of the keyboard, but where's the fun in that?

"Uh-uh, I got it."

"You never answered my original question, and hand me the bottle." He points to the bottle of Jack Daniels I brought over.

"What question?"

"Is. She. Hot?"

"You can't fuck her, Camden!"

Or I'll have to kill your ass.

"That's not what I asked." Camden roars with laughter. "But since you brought it up, let me meet her. I'll find out everything you need to know."

"Hell, no," I say through gritted teeth.

"Why? I'm a gentleman. I'm way better to women than you have ever been."

Unfortunately, he's right.

"You're a miserable asshole. Hell. No."

"Eh, I'll meet her at the club. When are you bringing

her? You gotta keep an eye on her, right? You'll have to bring her to the club at some point."

"Camden–" I'm barely holding it together. "You sound like your horny brother right now."

"I'm doing you a favor," he says sarcastically.

He's right about one thing, though. I can't run from this forever. It's time to man up. I pour myself a shot and make the tough decision.

"I'll go check on her and bring her to the club tomorrow, but I just want you and Cutter to be friendly to her. Put her at ease. Otherwise she's hands off. Don't let me have to tell you again."

"All I want to know is, Is. She. Hot?"

Fuck yes.

"She's family, asshole. I haven't even thought about it."

THIRTEEN

ELIZABETH

A BRISK KNOCK AT THE DOOR abruptly wakes me to a sunlight drenched room, and a laptop still in my bed that's about to conk out on less than five percent battery power. I fell asleep working in bed again.

I've actually been doing this for the last few days. Staying up because the freelance coders I'm able to afford all live in India, and we're on two completely opposite time zones. The only way we can chat live to troubleshoot is if I stay up, so that's what I do. Of course, this is driving Juliette completely insane. She doesn't understand what I do and why I need to stay up half the night to do it, and even if she did, all she cares about is feeding me.

"Come in," I say, completely hiding under my covers. I know it can only be her, but I look like death warmed over and my morning breath is lethal. I wouldn't want to kill her with it.

"Get up, Duchess."

I jump damn near out of my skin when I hear the deep familiar voice, and squeeze my legs tightly together when I peep my head from under the covers and notice Roman leaning against the inside of the door frame with his arms crossed in front of him, dressed in only a pair of black basketball shorts, and dripping in sweat. I can literally see every ridge and hard, sleek muscle in his forearms, biceps, chest, and torso. He must have zero body fat and the capability of lifting a Mack Truck. No wonder he oozes confidence and arrogance. How could he be anything but egotistical when he sees that every frackin' day in the mirror?

"I'm tired," I complain with the covers over my mouth.

"I bet," he snickers. "I heard that you've been working yourself to death up here."

"Did Juliette put you up to this? Why are you here?"

Where have you been?

"Not happy to see me?"

Hell, yes.

"Ugh."

I pretend I'm not elated to see him and pull the covers back completely over my head.

"Listen, Duchess. I'm not one for elephants in the room, so I'm just going to say it. I buried you in the backyard when we were kids. It was a shitty thing to do, but in my defense I was only ten. Let's move on."

That's the elephant in the room he wants to talk about? How about the fact that he was about two-seconds away from making me come right on the dance floor of a family party? Or the fact that I've been thinking about him nonstop since we met. I'm lusting after my own cousin!

So what we're not biologically related. It's still gross. I can hear my mother now.

Out of all the thousands of men in that city, you decide that you want to spread your legs for your cousin, Elizabeth? God, you're such a disappointment.

Then she'd make the sign of the cross and pray for my eternal soul.

"Don't make me pull those covers off," he warns, refusing to leave. "Get out of bed, nerd."

"Who are you calling–"

He whips the covers clear off of me, and I'm immediately exposed and freezing. Juliette still has the central air running, and I'm only wearing a very thin neon yellow tank top and a pair of pink and white polka dot panties. My stretched out, worn-out pair of panties. The ones you wear when you're almost completely out of clean underwear.

Crap.

I have no doubt Roman is used to slick, worldly women who only wear lace thongs and push-up bras and look like Victoria Secret models, the way I've seen women slobber over him. I'm sure I'm giving him a country mouse eyeful.

"Shit," I hear him mutter under his breath. "Where are your pajamas, Duchess?"

"This is what I sleep in, genius. Get out!"

All I can do is fuss at him to save face. I'm more angry at myself than anything he's said or done. Hell, I'm angry that I haven't washed clothes yet. I do own better looking underwear than this.

He runs his hand back and forth over the top of his head and exhales roughly.

"We're going out. Be ready in fifteen minutes. I'm not playing."

"I don't have time to play with you," I say back.

"Good, we're in agreement then."

"That's not what I–"

He closes the door sharply behind him, which makes the whole house rattle a little, and I throw my hands in the air in utter frustration.

"ASSHOLE!"

Not too long after, I hear a soft knock at the door and imagine he's about to tell me what he thinks about me calling him names.

"Oh, so you're knocking now?!"

"Elizabeth? It's me, sweetie."

Oh, God. It's Juliette. I pull the covers up to my chin so that she doesn't know that Roman just saw me practically nude, as well as to save her from my rancid breath. Where the heck is my pack of gum?

"Oops, Auntie."

She enters the room gingerly, like she's frightened that I'm going to throw a bottle at her head.

"Is it safe?"

"Ha, ha. I thought you were Roman again."

"He's just being a good cousin, honey. I know that I said that you wouldn't see him much around here, but he's just trying to get you out of the house for a while."

"So you put him up to this?"

"His father did." She holds her hands up like she's under arrest. "It wasn't me. I know how dedicated you are to your work."

Even though he's eerily quiet, Joseph has been nothing but super sweet to me since I've been here, and I can tell the way he is with Juliette, that he is possessive and protective by nature. Of course he would want someone to look out for me. He probably feels responsible for my well being since I'm currently living under his roof, but I just can't. Not with Roman.

"It's not like I don't know the city, Aunt Juliette. I've lived here for years. I went to Penn. I don't need a babysitter."

"Is this about Roman's prank when you were six,

because that was our fault, sweetie. We should've been keeping a better eye on things. He was just doing what boys that age do. Roman was always a handful."

"Auntie–"

"You're not going to stop saying aunt, are you?"

"Not to your face." I smile. "It just seems inappropriate to call you by your first name."

"My brother has always had a stick up his ass with formalities and stuff. I get it though. We were raised that way by your grandparents. It's just that I remember us both promising each other that our children would call each other by our first names. We thought the whole title thing was stupid when we were kids. We had to call anybody over the age of twenty-five aunt this or uncle that. Even our cousins. It was ridiculous."

"It's a shame that you and Dad can't figure out how to close this distance between the two of you. I'm pretty sure he misses you."

"What makes you think that?" she asks wistfully.

"Just a feeling."

"Well, maybe one day we'll clear the air. Having you here is actually a big step in the right direction."

"How does helping your homeless niece repair things between the two of you?" I chuckle.

"I don't know if ten years ago he would have ever allowed you in this house. He must be mellowing with age, or maybe because you're an adult now. Either way, it's progress."

I smile but wonder to myself what on earth could have happened to make my dad avoid his only sister for most of his adult life?

"Will you tell me what happened?" She exhales tiredly.

"Your father and Joseph have some issues."

"What issues?"

"They don't like each other. Your father didn't want me to marry him. He made me choose. I chose Joseph."

My father is many things, but making his sister choose between him and the man she loves sounds extreme even for him.

"Let me brush out your hair before you jump in the shower, Elizabeth. It's gorgeous. Just like your mom's."

"Okay."

"You know that Bobby and Philip are four and six years older than your father and me."

Uncle Bobby and Uncle Philip are Juliette and my dad's older brothers and are both lawyers for my grandfather's firm.

"Yes."

"That's why your father and I were so close, because we're only a year apart, but we also worshipped our big brothers. Your dad wanted to hang around them and be just like them, and I wanted to date all their friends. Joseph was one of those friends.

"I'm pretty sure your dad envisioned me with a nice guy my age from school or something. The whole family did. But Joseph didn't go to our school, and he wasn't from our town. He was from the inner city, rough around the edges, and he was older than me. No one wanted me with Joe, but your dad definitely took it the hardest."

"So he cut you off completely because of who you chose to love?"

"Not completely. If I was to ever be in any real trouble, I know that your father would be there in an instant. I've never doubted that. We just decided that we couldn't be in each other's lives in the same way that we had been. It just wasn't going to work. Your dad never respected our relationship."

"May I ask why you didn't become a lawyer?"

She stops brushing my hair for a moment. "Has your father talked about that?"

"Maybe once."

He definitely brought it up more than once. Blaming my uncle for her "downfall," as he called it.

"It wasn't because of Joseph if that's what he said."

"Well, you don't have any children, so I was just wondering what stopped you from–"

"I lost a couple of children, Elizabeth." She cuts me short. "Three miscarriages to be exact."

"Oh my gosh, I didn't know. I'm so sorry."

"It was a long time ago, sweetie. I just couldn't seem to carry any of my angels to full term."

Juliette silently finishes brushing out the last section of my hair. I feel like crap. I shouldn't have asked her all of those questions. Sometimes I amaze myself at how I often manage to say or do the wrong things at the wrong time. I have the worst timing.

"There you're all done." She pats my shoulder.

"TEN MINUTES!" I hear the sexiest, raspiest voice bark up the stairs to the both of us.

"Gosh, your cousin is bossy just like his dad. Those Masterson men." Juliette chuckles and shakes her head.

"You better get ready."

FOURTEEN

ELIZABETH

MY NEW COUSIN MAKES ME anxious. There are no ifs, ands, or buts about it. He's managed to shower, dress and smell absolutely amazing in less than fifteen minutes, and he's keeping a close watch on me out of the corner of his eye while he drives. Gosh, the man even drives with swagger. Looking sexy as hell as he leans slightly back in his seat with his left arm guiding the steering wheel and the right stretched across the back of my seat. His hand is so close to the back of my head, I find myself sitting here waiting for him to start running his fingers through my hair.

"Where are we going?" I ask nervously.

"By the art museum," he says in a serious tone.

I turn my head to look square at him. "That's where I used to live."

"I know. Joseph told me you still have a few boxes in the basement and that you haven't received your security deposit back yet?"

I pick up my iPhone and play aimlessly around with the arrangement of my apps. I'm embarrassed and a little annoyed that my uncle has sent Roman to handle business that is my responsibility without even consulting me. I wonder if my mother told them about everything that happened, because she clearly must have told my aunt and uncle something. Of course, even she doesn't know everything.

"Why do you call your father Joseph?" I ask, changing the subject.

"The same reason why Juliette wants you to call her Juliette. They don't want to feel like they're old enough to be somebody's father or aunt."

"But they clearly are."

"They sure as hell are, but what can you say to the delusional?"

We both laugh at the same time, and my eyes lock with his for a fleeting moment.

"Are you and Joseph close?"

"Not exactly."

"But you work together right?"

"Yes, but it's not like you're thinking."

"What am I thinking?"

"That I wanted to follow in his footsteps, be a part of the family business, or some shit like that."

"Then what is it like?"

"It's more like I didn't have a lot of options, and I took the simplest path."

"Seems like a profitable path, though. This is a very nice car, and I hear you live in some fancy apartment on Chestnut."

We were riding in a freshly washed, black Range Rover SUV with tan leather interior and some sort of navigation system that looked like it was designed by a NASA engineer. And I couldn't help but overhear Juliette bragging to a girlfriend on the phone the other day about how she's so proud of Roman, and how he lives in a great building with a doorman at his age.

"We already had money, Elizabeth," he says flatly.

"Your father did, but Juliette says that you earn your own money. That they don't give you a dime."

"Does money impress you?" I detect a tone from him that suggests that me liking money is a bad thing. Like perhaps I'm some sort of shallow person, when I'm far from that. I'm just impressed by his success. His and Joseph's.

Everything they've seemed to have accomplished. I want to be independent and an entrepreneurial success like they are. I want people to remember who I am, or at least what my contribution to this world was, and I certainly don't want to have to live in my aunt's guest room while I do it.

"There's nothing wrong with money, but that's not what motivates me if that's what you're asking."

"What motivates you?"

"The work that I do."

"What are you working on exactly?"

"I'm designing an app."

"Oh, that's cool," he says with a little disinterest. "A game?"

"No, it's a productivity app that will help match high school seniors and college students to scholarship money." I say with pride in my voice.

He looks mildly impressed. "You're smart."

I shrug my shoulders. "More like inspired. My parents didn't have the money to send me to Penn, or any college for that matter, but they made too much money to qualify for needs-based scholarships. So I had to figure things out on my own. I spent most of my junior year of high school online, in libraries and bookstores researching hundreds of scholarships. It was a nightmare, but it worked. I paid for my entire college education. Room and board. Even food."

"So you want to help others have an easier time finding scholarships?"

"Exactly. The money is out there, it's just the search for it which is brutal."

"That's fucking amazing."

I grin like a goofball. There's something about receiving Roman's seal of approval that makes me feel like doing a hundred cartwheels.

We ride by one of my favorite diners, and I know we're back in my old stomping grounds. I'm getting nervous, and I need to find a way to tell Roman the reason why without telling him everything. I don't like to talk about the attack. I've barely told Sloan or my parents what happened, so I sure as hell don't want to spill my guts to him.

Roman already notices my apprehension. Shit. My hair twisting always gives it away.

"What's wrong?"

"I don't think I'm going to get the security deposit back."

"Why?"

"The place needs painting, there's a hole in the wall of my bedroom, and I didn't really clean when I left."

His eyebrows squish together. "Back up. Why is there a hole in your bedroom wall?"

"A misunderstanding."

"Between?"

"Me and my ex."

Well, that's sort of the truth.

"What's his name?" he asks flatly. "The ex." I turn my head and catch Roman staring at me.

"Keep your eyes on the road please," I request.

"I got this. I was driving well before you got your period. Just give me the name."

Gosh, he can be so crude sometimes.

"I don't want to tell you."

"Why?"

"Because I get the feeling you might actually do something with the information if I give it to you."

He grins. "That's the idea."

"I handled it."

He growls under his breath.

"Listen, Elizabeth, I know that we don't know each other that well yet, but you're going to learn a couple of things about me very quickly. I'm an expert at handling shit, I don't like to ask things twice, and I don't accept the word no very often or very well."

Something about that very matter-of-fact statement makes my nipples tingle. I imagine he's very hard to say no to, and that I probably couldn't say the word very much at all to him. I probably wouldn't want to.

"I need the name. It's my third time asking," he warns.

"Ethan Anderson," I say reluctantly.

"See, was that so hard?" he asks with a grin while keeping his eyes on the road.

"I guess not," I say with an unintentional quiver in my voice.

Roman turns his head, looks at me and squints again. It's like his eyes are a bullshit meter.

"What aren't you telling me?"

I take a deep breath and just spit it out. Chances are my mom told Juliette or Joseph most of what she knows, anyway.

"I didn't have a fight with my ex. We were both attacked in my apartment. That's why there's a hole in the wall."

Roman quickly swerves the Range Rover over to the shoulder of the road. I can hear bits of gravel popping as we roll over them.

"What happened?" he asks with an eerie but deadly like calm.

"Why are you stopping?" I ask nervously.

"Talk." He hooks my chin with his pointer finger. "And I mean everything, Duchess."

Every time he calls me that, I can't breathe.

I lean my body into the passenger side door as I speak, wishing I could burrow myself even further. The fresh air from the window I cracked is whipping stray hairs around my face and they're sticking to my lips. I'd do just about anything right now to change the subject, but I know it's not going to happen. I can see that about him already. The steely determination across his face. He's waiting patiently for my story, and he's made it clear that he doesn't like to ask for things twice.

"My boyfriend was over ... Ethan. We were fooling around in my bedroom when we heard a loud crash in the front of my apartment."

I turn to look at Roman's face. He motions for me to continue.

"There were men in the house."

"How many?"

"Three."

"How do you know there were three for sure?"

"Because two had guns drawn on Ethan and one knocked me out. My head made the hole in the wall."

Roman grips the steering wheel tightly while drawing deep breaths, and I stop talking. There's an awkward silence between us now.

We're still sitting on the shoulder of the road and

Roman hasn't looked my way or spoken to me in over six minutes. I know it's been exactly six, because I've been paying close attention to the time on my phone. I don't know him that well, but his body language suggests that keeping quiet and giving him time to process what I said then let him calm down is the right approach.

"Is that why you're at my father's house?" he asks, finally breaking the silence.

"Yes, I couldn't stay in that apartment anymore. I just—"

"And where is ... Ethan?" he asks with disdain on his lips, although I don't know why. I haven't even told him about the drugs yet.

"His parents told me that he's in rehab in Arizona."

"So this was drug related?"

"I think so, but I didn't know he did drugs," I say in my defense. "Ethan is a swimmer and an athlete. He always told me that he'd never do drugs."

"Do you love him?"

"What?! No." That was a weird question.

"Is he still your boyfriend?"

You would think I'd have an emphatic answer of a "hell no" to that question, but it isn't that simple. I haven't spoken to Ethan since the incident. He hasn't called, texted, or even written me a frackin' letter. Even most of his friends are avoiding me. It's almost as if they blame me for what happened, when it's totally obvious that Ethan got knee deep into something that he brought to my doorstep not the other way around.

"Umm—"

Roman raises an eyebrow at that response but moves on.

"And so what did the men want from him? Money or drugs?"

"Drugs, I think. They said Ethan had something that belonged to them."

"Do you remember exactly what they said, Duchess?"

"The two with the guns didn't say anything. The one who knocked me out did all the talking. He said that Ethan was lying, that he was high on his shit right now."

"Did you say anything to them?"

"Not one word. He hit me when Ethan said he didn't know what they were talking about."

"And then you woke up and everyone was gone?"

"Yes."

This sounds even worse when I try to explain it.

"Ethan went to Penn with you?"

"Yes."

"Is he from here?"

"No, he's from Maryland but why? What are you going to do, Roman?" I panic a little. "I just want to put this whole thing behind me. Joseph should have never asked you to do this. It's my business and–"

"There's no way in hell Joseph knows about this. Trust me. He thinks all I'm doing is taking you to pick up the rest of your things. He knows something happened to you for you to leave your apartment so abruptly, but nothing like this. If you're worried that your parents told him what happened, they didn't, and they didn't tell Juliette. That's if your parents even know."

"They sort of know."

"Sort of?"

"They don't know about Ethan or the drugs. They just know I was attacked in my home. I guess they decided not to tell Joseph."

"Are you protecting that asshole?" he asks coldly.

"No, that's not it at all. I just wish you would let me

handle it, Roman."

"You're family, so your business is my business. Remember that. And what the fuck are you so worried about, anyway? I told you, handling shit like this is what I do for a living, and I do it well."

He steers the car back on the road ... pissed off.

"You feel me?" he asks.

I nod.

Roman is saying all the right things, all very assuring things, but I worry that he's looking at me in a new light. I'm not sure why his opinion even matters to me, but it does.

Maybe he thinks differently of me now. Maybe he feels sorry for me. Maybe he realizes that I'm dumber than a doornail, because let's be honest, only an idiot would miss the fact that her boyfriend was a frackin' drug addict, right?

"Is that it?" He points to the management office of my old building while he unknowingly pulls into a parking space directly in front of my old apartment.

Roman is dressed in a slightly loose vintage ringer tee and worn jeans with a different pair of black hard bottomed boots on. His tats are very much visible today, and his height and width make him appear even more formidable. His shirt softly hugs his solid edges, and I gaze in amazement at what I already know is a six-pack rippling underneath. With a core that strong, I can't help but daydream about how easy it must be for him to lift a woman up and flip her over.

Good grief, I have issues.

"The black door," I instruct. "Use the knocker. The bell doesn't work."

I move to open the passenger side door but Roman shuts me down with four simple words in an *I'm not bullshitting* tone of voice.

"Stay in the car."

I don't argue. I can feel the hostility rolling off of him like a dark thundercloud. I'm not even sure why he's so angry. The apartment manager didn't have anything to do with what happened, but I'm still worried because the apartment manager is an asshole, and Roman doesn't seem like he has a lot of patience for assholes.

Roman reaches inside the compartment area between the two front seats and pulls out a bag of plain M&M's. He rips the bag open, shakes a few in his palm, then tosses a few of the hard-shelled candies one by one in his mouth as he exits the car.

"Be right back," he says confidently.

He doesn't use the knocker, but uses one of his massive fists to pound on the door three times. My old apartment manager Owen answers the door with irritation across his face. His normal look.

"Can I help you?"

"I'm here to collect Elizabeth Hill's security deposit and the rest of her things. She has a couple of boxes in the basement."

"And you are?"

"The person who is here to collect Elizabeth Hill's security deposit and the rest of her things."

"Funny, but she needs to do it. I can't turn anything over to you legally. I don't know who you are."

"Are you a lawyer?" Roman snidely asks.

"Are you?" Owen retorts as his body stiffens, but Roman's body language remains the same.

Cool as a cucumber.

"Are you a cop?" Romans asks.

"ARE YOU?" Owen says in frustration. "Listen, dude, I don't have time for this."

Owen scans the area and spots me sitting in the car biting my nails practically down to the nubs.

"I see you, Miss Hill." He points in my direction. "And I highly suggest you forget about getting that security deposit back after the state you left my unit in."

"No, I highly suggest you shut the fuck up and go get what I asked for. I'm not going to tell you again," Roman responds.

I motion to get out of the car to try to talk some sense into Owen, but I stop when Roman speaks to me again. He doesn't even turn around when he says it. He doesn't need to.

"Stay in the car, Elizabeth."

So I release the door handle and stay put.

He pops another few candies in his mouth and speaks with a deadly calm to Owen, as if he's holding onto his last bit of restraint.

"My cousin is in that car. You see her, right? She is here for her security deposit of ... what is it again, Elizabeth?" he calls out.

"Nine hundred and fifty dollars," I answer meekly.

"Damn! Now that's a high ass security deposit. What is this the Trump Towers? Okay, so I'll need you to get nine hundred and fifty dollars cash and her remaining boxes. She doesn't need to get out of the car to sign anything, or talk to you, or whatever the fuck. That's why I'm here. Hand everything over to me in the next five minutes and we'll be square. You don't want to cooperate then we're going to have a major problem, because I didn't drive all the way over here to leave empty-handed."

Roman cracks his neck.

"You feel me, dickhead?"

FIFTEEN

ELIZABETH

TODAY IS TURNING INTO A full-blown crash course in Roman 101. I've learned that five minutes in Roman's world really means exactly that. It was five minutes on the dot when Owen handed over my security deposit in cash and the key to the storage garage. It shocked me that he even had that much cash in his possession. Who does that? Oh, wait ... I used to (*baha!*). Anyway, after he handed over the cash and the key, he went inside his apartment without another word and locked the door.

After Roman and I loaded my four plastic containers of treasures (photos, journals, sweaters and other trinkets) in the back of his Rover, we decide to stop for lunch. I suggest that we eat at Brown's Diner, one of Philadelphia's legendary last remaining family-owned diners and one of my favorite places on earth.

"You've eaten here before I take it?" he asks, noticing my excitement.

"All the time. Best five dollar lunch in the area."

"What the hell can you get for five dollars?"

"Don't be such a snob, rich boy. You're about to have the

best turkey burger and fries EVER." I smile. "My treat. Since I'm rich now too."

I fan a little of my money in his face when I notice an incoming text on my phone.

Roman chuckles and pauses before he asks his next question, "Who's that, moneybags?"

"It's Owen."

Roman's face turns icy.

"What the fuck does he want?"

"For me and my crazy ass cousin to never come around there again or he'll call the police."

"Is that right."

I laugh. "Well, you've got to admit. You were kind of over the top with him."

"I was fixing a very fucked up situation. He was trying to keep your money, and you were allowing him to speak to you like a piece of shit."

I gasp in mock shock. "Tell me how you really feel."

"I really feel like you have a horrible taste in landlords and definitely in men."

"I guess so. My last boyfriend was apparently a druggie, and I think I came pretty damn close to making out with my cousin in front of our entire family." I chortle a little at my attempt at a joke.

Roman is stock still.

I'm guessing he doesn't think my joke was that funny.

"So what else is on the agenda for today?" I ask, hoping to steer the conversation in another direction.

"I need to make a stop, then we're going home to change, and then out to The Lotus."

"The Lotus? Why would we go there?"

"I'm running it now."

"You're running it! I thought you were a business consultant."

"I am. I consult employees on how to run their clubs, among other things."

I shake my head no. "I don't want to go back to that nightmare on Elm Street."

"Nothing will happen to you as long as I'm there." He says confidently.

"And who pays you to run this club? No offense, but it doesn't look like your type of crowd."

"No offense taken, but it's not your crowd either, and the owner pays me."

I roll my eyes at his inferred insult.

"And who's the owner?"

"A silent investor. Any more questions about my business, Inspector Clouseau?"

"Nope." I cut my sloppy turkey burger into quarters and then pop a French fry into my mouth and chew. "Pass the ketchup."

"I don't know how you keep your girlish figure."

"Not used to eating with girls who eat real food, I take it?"

"Are you used to it? Your girlfriend doesn't look like she eats much."

"Sloan?" Of course he paid attention to Sloan's body. Every man does. Pervert.

"Yeah, her. I noticed her scrawny little ass on the floor of the club that night."

"So, it was Sloan you were looking at when you found us?" I try to ask nonchalantly as I dip a fry in my small pool of ketchup.

Roman takes a large bite of his burger. Chewing it while

silently observing me. He licks a bit of juice from the corner of his mouth, swallows, then smiles.

"I noticed only you the moment you entered the club, Duchess."

Our eyes lock.

"What do you mean? You saw me before the pepper spray?"

"Yep," he says simply.

I'm not sure what to say in response to this bit of new information. I don't know if I should say anything. We're supposed to be having friendly conversations. Distant cousins getting to know each other. I'm pretty sure that's what Juliette and Joseph had in mind by forcing Roman to babysit me, but I feel like almost every exchange between us is laced in subtle sexual subtext. I don't know. Maybe it's all in my head.

"So tell me about the stop you need to make today. Is it for your job?"

"Pretty much."

"About the club?"

"No, this is a different job. I have a client that's being blackballed by MTV. She wants to present at the awards show, but they're freezing her out."

"Wow, that sounds so interesting. So what can you do about it?"

"Well, it's my job to convince the powers that be to change their minds about her."

"Who is it, Roman? Tell me!"

"Absolutely not." He smiles and tweaks my nose. "You wouldn't want me to lose my job now, would you?"

"I thought MTV was in New York?"

"The person I need to speak with is here for a few days."

"And you're going to let me tag along?" I ask excitedly.

"Not inside, Duchess. You'll sit in the car like a good girl and wait for me." He gives me one of those signature panty-dropping smirks of his, and honestly, I think my crotch is on fire ... in a good way.

In the best way possible.

IT DOESN'T TAKE LONG FOR US to leave the diner and arrive to our next destination. We're in front of a mammoth but beautifully designed slate concrete building with lots of glass and stainless steel on the lobby floor. There's no name on the building, just an address in large, polished stainless letters, which rests above the set of double glass doors.

1907.

There's an older man with a paunch belly standing in front of the building dressed in a maroon short coat with brass buttons who seems to stand at his post as the doorman with pride. I notice that he recognizes Roman and am surprised that he addresses my tatted up cousin with nothing but respect instead of revulsion or fear.

"Going in, Mr. Masterson?"

"What's up, Tyson. I need to run upstairs for a minute. Floor 15. Also, I have a young lady in the car who I need you to keep an eye on."

He lowers his head to look inside the car and gives me a thousand-watt smile.

"Pleasure."

"Hello," I respond brightly.

"You'll stay in the car?" Roman grins.

"What's with you and making me stay in cars? Just hurry up, Masterson."

It's the first time I've called him something other than his name. Not quite a nickname like the one he's given me, but something other than Roman. I think he likes it, because he smirks as he exits the car. As the man Tyson opens the door for him, he runs back to the car and signals for me to roll down the window.

"I forgot something."

He reaches into the middle compartment and grabs a couple of M&M's. Tosses them down his throat.

"Give me fifteen minutes."

"No worries," I assure him.

I'm kind of enjoying hanging out with Roman today, although a part of me is itching to go home and get some work done. I really need to get back to researching more scholarships and adding them to my database. It's important that I create the most complete list that I can, so I'm ready for my pitch when the opportunity strikes, and the only person who I can depend on to get it done is me.

For the last four months I've been looking for an angel investor, so I can finally hire a full-time coder who works specifically for me and can get my application to where it needs to be. The freelancers I've been able to hire here and there are definitely knowledgeable, but I can only hire them when a few dollars clear up on one of my credit cards, so I don't have someone working consistently on the coding.

I feel pretty confident that once I have that last piece in place, and my beta product is excellent, I'll have a better chance of succeeding in the highly competitive app market-place. Maybe even get some good press. Luckily, I have my smartphone and a pad and pen in my bag right now. That's all I need to continue my research in the car, while I wait for Roman to finish his business.

I'm busy for about all of ten minutes when there's a rap

on the window. It's a woman. An exquisite, slender woman dressed in a rather conservative blush colored pencil skirt and blouse with nude pumps. I notice Tyson looking over at us, but he says nothing, he just pulls out an old flip phone and busies himself making a call or sending a text.

I roll the window down.

"Can I help you?" I ask the woman.

It literally takes her one second before she tosses an open bottle of spring water into my face. Now I'm soaking wet, and I don't know what the hell just happened or why it happened. That's when Tyson approaches the car and escorts the woman over to the sidewalk firmly by her upper arm.

"You are trespassing on private property, miss. You need to leave before I have you arrested."

She doesn't say a word in response, but she refuses to move any further. Crossing her arms in front of her and clenching her jaw. It's clear that she's waiting for something ... or someone.

"Are you crazy?!" Is all I manage to yell out through the window at her, while I grab a couple of napkins out of the glove compartment and wipe myself down. That's when I see Roman walking furiously through the lobby towards the doors, and it all clicks together for me. She's waiting for him.

He immediately notices my sopping wet face and shirt and then starts walking towards the woman with malice all across his face. It's none of my business. She obviously is one of his lovers, but I can't help but eavesdrop. I'm so ridiculously nosy when it comes to this man. Plus, she threw frackin' water at me like some trollop on a reality show.

"What are you doing here, Louise? We discussed this."

"I never agreed to anything. I'm not some whore you met off the street, Roman. I deserve better than this."

"You deserve exactly what you got. Total honesty. I don't do seconds. What don't you understand about that?"

"Who is she then?"

She points directly at me.

"Someone you shouldn't have fucked with."

Tears start to swell in the woman's eyes, and I'm feeling a bit embarrassed for her. What's worse is she looks over at me and catches me seeing her tear up, which is probably making everything a hundred times worse for her.

"YOU ARE A FUCKING WASTE OF MY BREATH, ROMAN MASTERSON!"

I was right.

The woman cries hysterically and literally foaming at the mouth. She's totally irate and out of control. Not like her heart has been broken, but more like she's had it up to here with men doing her dirty. Of course, if she hadn't tossed a bottle of water in my face, I might have more sympathy for her.

If Roman has this effect on a woman after one night, I think I should be relieved that I totally dodged that bullet. I most certainly would rather be his cousin. Okay, maybe not, but you know what I mean.

He walks away and says nothing else to the woman, which is a relief, because in another minute I think she would have pulled a gun on him or something. After jumping back in the car and nodding a good bye to Tyson, he turns to me as we pull off, his body shaking with laughter.

"You're wet."

"You think this is funny?!" I screech.

Then I break into laughter too, and now we are both in hysterics. I couldn't help it. My shirt was sopping wet, because he wouldn't give that poor woman seconds. This day was turning out to be a super funny adventure.

"I'm sorry about that. Her bank is literally two blocks away."

"Her bank?"

"She manages the federal credit union down the block."

"That crazy woman is a bank manager?"

"I only deal with classy women, baby," he jokes.

"Obviously."

He laughs again, and I have to admit that I'm starting to love watching Roman laugh. He doesn't do it a lot, but when he does it's completely addicting. His eyes crinkle at the corners, his mouth turns up on one side, and I get to see that amazing dimple again.

"So you don't do seconds?" I ask with curiosity.

"Not really."

"What does that mean exactly?"

"It means that I don't like to sleep with a woman more than once. They get too attached. You just saw it with your own eyes."

"You slept with her once? Really?" I ask incredulously.

"All facts." He grins. "Imagine how'd she stalk my ass if I gave it to her again."

I roll my eyes.

"You're such a pig, Masterson."

He laughs heartily.

WE HAD A LITTLE TIME TO KILL BEFORE we needed to change clothes for the club, so Roman decided to drive me around parts of the city that I'd never seen. During college, I'd spent most of my time in my one little corner of the world. On campus and very close by. I hadn't ventured out to other parts of the city. There was no need to, in my opinion.

We drove by what he explained was his former elementary school in a rundown part of town that looked like it was probably a pleasant neighborhood once upon a time. You could tell there were a few families on various blocks still trying to maintain their homes, but with limited funds. Roof shingles were askew, paint was peeling, and the concrete steps needed a redo, but the grass was also freshly cut and fresh red geraniums were planted in pots in the front of many of the houses.

When Roman points to the building where he learned the alphabet and his times tables, I'm shocked. There isn't enough landscaping in the world to make his elementary school look inviting. It looks like a massive stone and brick prison. I can't imagine any child entering that building every day and feeling optimistic about life. I feel like seeing it explains his rough edges and quick temper.

"That's big," I comment, not wanting to say what I really feel.

"Too big. There were a lot of kids that didn't get along, because this wasn't really their neighborhood. They were being bused in from other parts of the city. I only lived two blocks from here."

"What was wrong with that?"

"Big class sizes. No individual attention. Lots of fighting."

"So where'd your mom meet Joseph?" I ask curiously.

"Joseph's from the neighborhood, too. In fact, he went to this same school when he was a kid."

I'm surprised by that, and now I'm wondering where on earth people like my uncles met someone like Joseph.

"Oh."

"My parents knew each other from the neighborhood when they hooked up. It wasn't a romance. It was him getting his shit off a couple of times, and for my mom it was about having a baby before her biological clock blew up. She knew him, she trusted him, and mostly she was right to trust him. He did more than most of the babies' daddies from the neighborhood ever did. He always sent money every month and a gift at Christmas."

Roman says the last part with some bite to his voice. I guess that must have been all Joseph managed to do for most of his life. Send money.

"You didn't see him much growing up, I take it?" I ask, already knowing the answer.

"He would come around once in a while, but my mother has a lot of issues. Ones that Joseph didn't have a lot of patience for. That's why I eventually ended up living with him."

"Do you talk to your mother much now?"

"No."

I think I see a flash of pain in his eyes.

"Oh."

"I suppose your parents were very hands on out in the 'burbs."

"Yeah, I guess so."

"There's no need to be ashamed of it, Elizabeth. It's cool that your parents gave a shit. "

"Are you angry with your mom or Joseph?"

"No," he says again shortly. He obviously doesn't want to talk about this, so I leave it alone.

I notice a large sign that is advertising a palm reading for ten dollars, and I beg Roman to stop. I considered getting a reading online once, but I'd rather have a live in person experience.

"Roman, let's stop there."

"For what?"

"I want a reading."

"A reading? You do know that these people are frauds, right?"

"No, I most certainly do not know that. The lady on the Long Island Psychic is real."

"Are you kidding me right now, magna cum laude?"

"Summa cum laude."

"My bad but that makes it even worse. You've got to be kidding about wanting this reading."

"No, I'm not kidding. I want to get a reading."

"Palm readings are the ultimate hustle. You're just itching to spend that money in your pocket, aren't you?"

He parks the car.

"You're getting out too?" I ask.

"Uh ... yes. Someone needs to make sure you don't spend all your damn money in there."

"Will the car be okay?" I whisper.

"Why are you whispering?" He laughs at me. "You watch too many movies. The car will be fine. Let's go."

An olive-skinned woman who doesn't appear to be too much older than me, dressed in a long orange and gold maxi dress with spaghetti straps, greets us at the door.

"Welcome. Would you like a reading?"

"Yes, *I* would."

"Who's first?" She gives Roman an approving once over from head to toe. Even the palm reader wants in his pants. It never stops.

"I'm just watching." He gives me an I told you so look, but I'm not swayed. I'm still a believer. The fact that she wants in his pants doesn't make her a fraud. It just makes her human.

"Ok, then, have a seat at the round table behind that curtain, miss."

I give Roman a wink and make my way behind the curtain. The room is not exactly what I envisioned a palm reader's place to look like. I imagined lots of colorful, flowing drapery, candles and incense burning when in actuality it had more of a low key, calming energy.

There are pictures of sunrises and waterfalls on the walls. Natural wood shelving with tarot cards, candles, and other trinkets for sale. An indoor waterfall sits in the room's corner with a large wooden bowl at the base of it filled with cash, and a recording of a Native American flute is playing through a speaker hanging in the corner. It's very relaxing and spa like.

"May I have your hands, please?"

The woman holds my hands, palm side up and rubs her thumbs back and forth across the center of my palms. It tickles, but I try to hold still, because she is as serious as a heart attack about it.

"Something big is in the works for you. Something you've been working towards a long time."

Ding! Ding! Ding! I'm sold already.

"Yes," is all I reply. Being careful not to give her any details. I want to know what she sees and not what I want her to see.

"It's going to happen soon, and it's going to happen fast; and there will be decisions you are going to need to make in order for it to work out long term."

"Okay."

"He will be one of those decisions."

"Who?"

"The man outside."

"Are you sure?"

What does Roman have to do with my business? This is where she's starting to lose me, because I think she assumes that he's my boyfriend or something. An obvious mistake to make, but a mistake nonetheless.

She lifts her head from my palms and looks directly into my eyes. "I am sure."

"What about my love life?" I wonder if she sees anything about Ethan.

She pauses for a moment as she holds my hands, then looks at me curiously.

"He will be the love of your life."

"Who?"

"The man outside."

I almost laugh.

"Not likely," I mutter under my breath.

"But be careful, because the passion between you two may consume you."

I tune much of what she says out after that. I've been successfully rattled. I don't think the reader is a complete fraud, because I feel (or at least hope) she was spot on about my business, but her comments about Roman have thrown me off kilter.

She instructs me to leave my offering, instead of a payment, in the bowl at the base of the waterfall. Then she recommends that I purchase a homemade candle to burn for further reflection. I've got the money in my pocket, so I say what the hell and purchase a vanilla and lavender soy candle for twenty bucks.

Roman stands as I exit the room, and he looks relieved that it's over.

"How was it?"

"Interesting."

"How much did you spend?"

"Thirty dollars."

"For a ten-dollar reading?"

He throws a friendly hook arm around my neck as we walk to the car, and it feels so frackin' good. I pray that my attraction towards him doesn't grow any stronger than it already is, but I think I already know the answer to that.

"Did the hustler tell you something life shattering behind the curtain?" he asks smugly.

It's complicated.

SIXTEEN

ROMAN

"WE NEED TO TALK."

Those are four words most men usually dread hearing from a woman, but for me there is nothing worse than when those four words come out of my father's mouth.

Why?

Because I know that whatever follows those words is never going to be a good thing for me.

"About?" As if I don't already know.

"Elizabeth."

Shit.

SEVENTEEN

OVER AN HOUR LATER, AFTER our day together, a very shower damp Roman is standing in the doorway of my bedroom in nothing but a towel wrapped around his waist, holding my favorite hot pink bra and black lace panties in his hands. I'm terribly embarrassed because I don't make a habit of allowing men to touch my lingerie, but because I've been slacking on doing laundry, I had to hand wash a few things in the bathroom sink.

Of course my traitorous eyes are magnetically drawn to Roman's bare sculpted pecs, lean torso, and his well-defined abs, but his lack of boundaries infuriates me enough to snap out of it. I'm freshly showered and sitting up in bed in only a long t-shirt and panties with my laptop on my lap. He needs to stop dropping by my room whenever he feels like it, and he definitely needs to wear more damn clothes.

"Why don't your bra and panties match?"

I just need to breathe through his totally inappropriate question, as I try to divert my eyes away from what I imagine is under that towel.

One. Two.

Three.

"Women's underwear is expensive," I explain. "I buy things on sale, so they don't always match." An honest answer, but delivered in a slightly patronizing tone. "Matching underwear is a frivolous expense for women who can afford it. Understand, rich boy?"

"Your coke-sniffing boyfriend couldn't buy you any matching underwear?"

That was a low blow.

"I'm sorry, but what crawled up your ass in the last sixty minutes, and why are you even taking a shower here? Don't you have your own place, pervert?"

Roman flashes me a devilish smirk. One he must use that wobbles a woman's knees upon sight, because it was working wonders inside my panties. I rub my legs together under the sheets of my bed like a cricket in an effort to stop the buzz that is slowly building between them.

"I was using the bathroom in my father's house, and your skivvies were hanging on the shower rod for anyone to see and touch. It was almost as if you wanted someone to see them, cousin."

Roman chucks my favorite bra and panties across the room, and they land on top of my lampshade. I wonder if I let them stay there and sizzle a bit, if I could get him arrested for arson.

He's in a stinky mood.

"And there's definitely nothing perverted about touching your itty bitty bra and granny panties."

"You're such an ass sometimes."

"Not as big as the one you're lying on. Speaking of that. Why are you in the bed? You're supposed to be getting dressed. We're going out in thirty damn minutes. Leave the coding or whatever the hell it is you do alone for one night, nerd."

This jerk!

He's been missing in action for thirteen days (yes, I'm counting), and then today he just whirls into my life like a hurricane. Forcing me to hang out with him all day; bossing me around; threatening the landlord with bodily harm (although I appreciated the end result). Standing in my doorway, giving me attitude, like we've known each other all our lives. It's infuriating; and possibly addictive. I'm afraid that I'm liking his brand of crazy a little too much.

"I repeat. What crawled up your ass?"

"I'm just wondering why you're in the bed talking to some dude in New Delhi when you should be getting ready to go out. You've known all day that we're going out."

"All right already! I'll be ready in thirty minutes."

"Not thirty; fifteen minutes."

"What! Why?"

"Because none of us can eat in this house until you do. Juliette insists that we wait for her precious niece to come down before anyone can have a bite of food."

"We just ate, you frackin' Neanderthal! You can't possibly be hungry."

"Frackin'?" Roman lets out a thunderous laugh. "Did you just say frackin'?"

"What of it?" I say defensively.

"That's a made up curse word from Battlestar Galactica if I recall. Damn, you really are a nerd."

He's laughing so hard now that I swear I just saw a tear roll down the side of his face. He's seriously so annoying. I don't know why I even bother.

"Only another fellow nerd would recognize the term, asshole," I say with venom.

"Unless I was fucking a nerd who used to watch the SciFi channel on the weekends, and I picked it up from her," he counters.

"And how would a man who doesn't do seconds know what a woman was watching on TV over the weekend?"

"Food, Duchess," he responds in an obvious attempt to avoid that particular question. "I want to eat dinner before we go. Juliette made pot pies."

I grin, because I know I won that verbal sparring.

"All right, I'll be there in fifteen or maybe I won't. Maybe skipping a meal will do wonders for my ass since you seem so concerned about the size of it."

"Only missing one meal will not do the trick, cousin," he laughs out loud.

I really want to laugh too, but I refuse to give him the satisfaction of thinking that he's funny. So I do what any immature kid would do and look for the closest thing I can find (one of my UGG boots) and throw it as forcefully as I can at Roman's beautiful buzzed-cut head. Not the most effective weapon since they're made out of soft sheepskin, but it was better than nothing.

I would have hit him square between the eyes if he hadn't suddenly blocked it and batted it down like some sort of ninja. Of course he would have quick reflexes. Why wouldn't he? He's built just like a frackin' UFC fighter.

"You missed," he sticks out his tongue at me like the four-year-old I'm learning he can be too. I roll my eyes at him, and then suddenly something in the air changes.

Without warning, Roman strolls inside my room, shuts my door, and sits on the edge of the bed next to me. It was easy to hold my own when he was standing in my doorway, but now that he's literally two inches away from my semi-dressed body, I feel less sure of myself.

He gently touches a few strands of my hair, curls them around his fingers, and uses them to softly brush across his bottom lip.

I'm staying stock still.

It's the second time that I am able to see his entire tattoo, but this time around, I study it. He's so close to me, I can't help it. It's a beautiful tribal mosaic that swirls and curves around the length and width of his back and travels up the left side of his neck where it ends. You can tell that it was painstakingly designed and executed, and frankly it takes my breath away. That and the fact that he is touching me again.

"What are you doing?" I ask nervously while I quickly sit up straighter and pull my massive head of hair out of his hands and into the neatest top-knot I can. That was a mistake, though.

When I lift my arms, the movement raises my breasts up higher and directly in his line of vision. He gazes almost hungrily at my breasts, then looks back to my face with a thirst in his eyes that makes me shiver.

"Duchess—"

"Yes?" I immediately respond.

He stops as we both look across at ourselves in the mirror above my dresser. Both of us very still as a moment of silence passes between us. I can no longer hold his stare and am looking away from him when he suddenly pulls my knotted hair free.

"I like your hair down."

My panties are sopping wet now.

He wraps his hand around the base of my throat and uses his thumb to slowly stroke my bottom lip. Back and forth until my lips part.

He pushes his thumb inside my mouth, and I foolishly

shut my eyes and then close my lips around it and suck. I didn't mean to, it was just a natural reaction to the fire he is stoking inside of my body.

"Lie down, Duchess," he says closely by my ear.

He picks up my laptop and places it gently on my nightstand. His hand begins to slowly drag down my neck and to my chest where he rubs one of my nipples between his thumb and forefinger. All his movements are painstakingly slow, fluid and careful. He knows a woman's body, and I can tell that he is trying to study mine.

When he moves to the left nipple, the sensation I feel multiplies tenfold because that breast has always been more sensitive than the other. Now my hips rise like they have a mind of their own. Moving. Flexing. Begging for Roman to relieve me of the ache that is snowballing between my legs.

He rolls and tugs, rolls and tugs, until he hears a slight gasp from me. Then his hand continues on its downward path. And I realize immediately that this is the moment right here. The moment where I have a decision to make. If I allow him to slide his hand inside my panties where I know he's headed, there will be no coming back from that.

Think, Elizabeth. This is your cousin.

But I say nothing, and I allow his hand to slide right in. It's like a water slide down there, which seems to emphatically delight him by the self-satisfied grin spread across his face.

"You're so fucking wet for me."

"Masterson—" I protest unconvincingly.

"This is what's going to happen, Duchess," he cuts me off. "You're going to spread your legs, come for me twice, and then we're going to eat a pot pie and head out to the club. You feel me?"

Before I can open my mouth to say another word, his

mouth captures mine in a mind blowing, frantic kiss while he simultaneously slides one of his thick fingers between my folds and then inside me. It feels so tremendously good that I want to smack somebody. I've never been touched like this before. He's playing my body like an instrument, and I'm not sure what kinds of animalistic sounds are coming out of my mouth, but they're in total response to the pure ecstasy I am feeling right now.

"Spread wider," he commands. So I do.

He uses his thumb next to rub back and forth over my clit while still pumping both of his thick fingers in and out of my pussy and the next thing I know; I see a million frackin' stars burst into a pure blinding white light, and I let out a shriek that all the neighborhood dogs can probably hear on the next block.

"Shhh," he chuckles with his lips against my mouth. "I still owe you another one."

I'm tingly and flushed, and frankly I don't think I can take another Masterson orgasm. Not quietly anyway.

"Wait—" I beg quietly.

Why I thought he would listen is beyond me.

He flips me over in one quick motion (which is damn impressive considering the size of my child bearing hips), smacks me on the right ass cheek, and then orders me around again.

"All fours, baby."

There's something about being on all fours in front of a man that makes me feel extremely vulnerable. Maybe it's because I can't see his eyes and know what he's thinking (as if I really could know for sure). Or maybe it's because I can't imagine what the view is like from back there. Needless to say, I've never done it, and I don't know why the hell I'm propping myself up right now.

"I've never—"

"Shhh," he quiets me. "I'm just going to lick that pussy clean, but you have to be a good girl and keep still and quiet for me ok?"

Oh. My. God.

If he keeps talking to me like that, I'm going to come right the frack now. He won't have to even touch me again.

"Can you do that?" he asks again.

I nod my head.

Then he slaps my ass again. Harder.

"Oww!"

"Can. You. Do. That?" he asks again with a growl.

"Yes."

"Good girl. All fours. Knees wider."

I don't know if I can do this...

"Wider. Don't hide from me."

I spread my knees wider and inhale a deep breath. Praying that Juliette doesn't walk in on this clusterfuck. Suddenly all I feel is warmth. The warm strokes of Roman's tongue stroking my clit up and down, and back and forth with precision and care. He's not as urgent as before. This time he's taking his time, and it's making the climb all that more torturous. I'm tense yet turned on at the same time. I feel super exposed in a way that I've never been before, but it feels amazing.

"That's a sweet pussy," he mutters in between licks. "This time I want you to try and hold off coming, Duchess."

"What?" Is he kidding me?

"I want you to wait until I give you permission."

My legs quiver as I feel the tension swirling inside of me, getting ready to burst. My breaths become shallow as I'm pretty sure I'm about to come.

Then he stops.

He blows a few warm breaths in between my legs, kisses me on my inner thigh, and starts talking again. But I don't want him to talk. I want him to continue on with what the hell he was doing, before I have to pin his ass down and sit right on top of his face.

"We have a situation," he announces, but I have zero idea what he's talking about.

"A situation?" I pant.

"Yes."

He's right. We do have a situation. A very bad one. This is my chance to stop this before it goes any further. I am acting like a total whore right now. I'm getting eaten out by my aunt's stepson while she prepares pot pies downstairs! Am I the one on drugs?

I try to turn myself over, because the first order of business would be to get my ass out of Roman's face, but he uses his brute strength to hold me in place and he takes another smack at my ass. This time it's a little closer to my pussy, and I squeeze my eyes shut for a moment while I wait for the feeling of utter ecstasy to pass.

"Masterson, we can't," I say breathlessly.

"I know," I hear the gruff regret in his voice.

Then his mouth returns in between my legs and he takes a long, deep pull of my clit with his lips while shoving both of his fingers back inside me, and I explode.

My hands fist the sheets of my bed and my entire body convulses as I use every ounce of strength in me to not scream bloody murder. It was the most excruciatingly powerful orgasm I've ever had. By my hand or another's. So good that I had to catch myself when I felt a tear form in the corner of my eyes. Having to keep silent during my orgasm probably made it that much more raw and over-whelming.

He growls as he turns me back over. "I asked you to wait."

"I couldn't!" I protest while panting out of breath.

"You'll do better next time," he says.

And that's when I realize that the palm reader was right. If I'm not careful, this man is going to utterly consume me.

ME: I need you to meet me somewhere in like an hour.

Sloan: Where?

Me: The Lotus.

Sloan: I thought it was closed.

Me: It's open again and Roman is the manager.

Sloan: I don't believe it. I'm stunned shitless.

Me: I'll explain later. I need you to come because I don't want to go:(

Sloan: So why are you going?

Me: Call it family pressure.

Sloan: I'll be more than happy to get that particular family obligation completely off your back:)

I told Sloan the minute I found out that Roman was my cousin, which she found totally tragic and hilarious in the same breath. Tragic for me that I'd never get to know him in a "biblical" way. Hilarious because of the stories she'd get to tell their grandchildren about how they met.

What I haven't revealed to Sloan is how my attraction towards Roman has grown by leaps and bounds since we first met that night at The Lotus. Every interaction between us pulls me in deeper, especially the one we just had. And there's no way in hell that I'm going to tell Sloan that I damn near cried after my cousin gave me the best damn orgasm of my life.

That's just something a girl needs to keep to herself.

EIGHTEEN

ELIZABETH

CLUB LOTUS HAS CHANGED significantly in the last few weeks. The intricate details which made the club beautiful are even more noticeable now that the club has been cleaned from top to bottom. I love the curves and swirls of the crown molding in the club. It makes me imagine a time in history when visiting the bank was obviously a luxurious experience. Something only reserved for the wealthiest of Philadelphia society. Nothing like the cold, sterile banks we use today.

Then there are the contemporary touches that make The Lotus just as beautiful. The modern crystal chandeliers which hang like sparkling pendulums from the twenty foot high ceilings are a happy marriage of old world meets twenty-first century. They have been polished to a clear sparkle, and the exotic mahogany wood bars have been buffed to a spit shine. A simplistic, pared down stage has been built by the south wall, and I notice how even the lighting is softer on the dance floor now. No more eye squinting strobe lighting.

There doesn't seem to be that same homogeneous group

of middle class corporate types dancing their cares away either; ordering bottles like they're planning on getting good and wasted on the finest liquor money can buy, because they hate their bosses. Instead, I notice that there is a more eclectic group of people, sitting, talking, drinking and having a good time, and I swear that I can recognize several faces chatting at a table near the DJ booth. I'm just not sure from where.

After taking a good look at my new and improved surroundings, I notice that there is a new elevated seating area at the top of a large curved staircase which features a large, oblong wooden coffee table and several plush chairs surrounding it. These are definitely new and they're all colored blood red. It's from that area that an attractive petite woman with shredded jeans and a tight graphic tee on whistles down to Roman through her teeth to get his attention. Roman responds with a nonchalant head nod to her and the two men she's sitting with. Then he moves in their direction.

He doesn't say much to me, in fact he's only grunted a few words to me since we left home, and his silence makes me feel simultaneously embarrassed and ashamed of what's happened between us. I suppose he regrets what's occurred as much as I do which would explain the whole I'm not saying shit to you Elizabeth thing. Maybe this is how he treats all the women that he's been intimate with. Which would pretty much explain why that pretty bank manager threw water in my face today.

Now I'm looking to see if Sloan has made it here yet, because I don't know if she'll see me seated in this section. It's pretty dimly lit, and I don't want to be stuck by myself with Roman and his friends all night. I'm sick of him being all hot and cold. He was in a bad mood when he came to my room tonight, then he expertly got me off twice, and now he's moody again. Unfortunately, eating Juliette's scrumptious chicken pot pie and giving me two orgasms didn't solve his bad-ass mood. Like I said, I'm assuming that his crappy disposition has something to do with the regret that he feels about what we did earlier. I feel the same way, but you don't see me taking it out on him. The jackass.

When we arrive to our seats, I'm struck by how attractive the two men are that are waiting for us. They look very much alike, so I assume they must be related, and they're both staring at me like they already know exactly what I'm wearing underneath my clothes. The woman extends her hand and speaks to me first.

"Hi, I'm Jade. This is Cutter and Camden. You must be the new cousin."

Interesting that he's mentioned me but I don't know one single thing about them.

"That's me. It's nice to meet you all. I'm Elizabeth."

Roman sits down next to Jade and across from me. Maybe that's why he's so on edge suddenly. Maybe she's his girlfriend, or at least another one of his friends with benefits. The guy named Camden is watching me carefully, and I blush because he's making me a bit uncomfortable on top of the fact that he's so good looking.

"Would you like a drink?" Camden asks while he waves down a waitress.

"She'll have a glass of merlot," Roman interjects abruptly.

Jade takes a hesitant glance at Roman and then another back to me.

"You like wine?" she asks, surprised.

"Yeah, I can't really stomach the hard stuff. Thank you,

Camden, but actually I'll have a glass of cabernet." Roman rolls his eyes.

"Well, that's too bad, because we do shots." The other hot guy named Cutter smiles brightly and says. "And we do 'em all night."

"I'll pass," I chuckle.

"She'll have one," Roman says, and this time I give him a hard look. What the hell is he doing?

He shrugs his shoulders with indifference. "You need to relax a little, cousin."

I want to kick him.

"I can speak for myself thank you very much."

He mutters something under his breath, only loud enough for him to hear.

"So what do you do, Elizabeth?" Jade asks after giving Roman another long look. I think she wants to smack him too.

Please do.

"I'm an app developer. I went to Penn for computer science."

I almost laugh at how I made myself sound ridiculously way more impressive than I really am. I need to take a course in small talk.

"Damn!" Cutter says. "Smart and you look like that. You ever think about the benefits of marrying young? I'm a fantastic lover." He flirts. I smile back.

I can see already that there's something a bit endearing about this guy.

Roman starts to tap the heel of his foot nervously when Jade places the palm of her hand firmly on his knee to calm it. She definitely must be a friend with benefits. I don't know why I'm so surprised, although he didn't mention anything about a Jade until we were well on our way over here.

I wonder if she knows that Roman rarely talks about her, that he has some crazy-ass bank manager stalking his ass, and that he just ate me out an hour ago. I wonder what would happen if I told her all of that interesting information. Of course, I'm too chicken shit to ever do that.

Sloan: I'm here. Where are you?

Me: At the top of the staircase

Sloan: Is the father of my future kids there?

Me: Whatever and yes. But I think he has a date.

Sloan: I brought some reinforcements with me

Me: Who?

Sloan: Carla. Tiny. Jagger.

Me: OMG!

Sloan: Thank me later, bitch.

"A couple of my friends are on there way up here. I hope that's okay," I say excitedly.

I make sure to stand by the banister and wave my hand so Sloan can see me.

"What friends?" Roman asks suspiciously.

"Sloan and a few friends from school."

"Oh right ... the Glamazon."

"What does that mean?" Cutter asks with interest.

"Tall, thin, the usual," Roman says.

"Hot?"

It's a knee jerk reaction, but I look up to Roman to see how he'll answer the question. He looks me straight in the eyes with little expression across his face when he replies to Cutter.

"Absofuckinglutely."

If he said it to piss me off, it worked. I look at Jade to see if he's hurt her feelings at all, but I can't really read her. I think I'm the only one who's more irked by the comment, and I hate that I even care. So what he made me come like an hour ago. That doesn't mean anything. In fact, I've got to get a grip. I can't just make out with my cousin and think that it means something. That it's ok. It's not. That's why I'm counting on one particular reinforcement Sloan brought to help me shake this whole Roman Masterson spell I'm falling under.

Jagger Reed is another graduate from the university swim team and was probably Ethan's primary competition for a spot on the Olympic team. He's built like the quintessential All-American boy. A tall and broad swimmer's body, eyes that shine, and a crooked smile. If I could do things all over again, Jagger would've been the guy I went out with in school. Not Ethan. He is the only one of Ethan's friends who called to check on me after the attack. Everyone else has been avoiding me like the plague, as if I am the reason that Ethan has been kicked out of swim club and in rehab. I'm sure Sloan asked him along because she knows I've always had a little crush on him. Long before Ethan.

"You said friends as in plural," Camden says. "Who else is coming?"

"Some friends I went to school with. A girl from our old dorm; her name is Tiny. And a guy we know named Jagger." Roman frowns.

"Hi y'all." Sloan waves as the three of them make their way up the staircase. She looks amazing as usual in a simple ribbed white tank top, skinny jeans, thin gold hoops and heels. I give her and Tiny a quick hug and offer a smile to Jagger.

"Damn! Your legs go on for days," Cutter exclaims.

Sloan grins.

"And you are?" she asks, amused.

"Your future."

She giggles. I roll my eyes (to myself). I thought I was his future just a minute ago.

"I'm Sloan, this is my old college roommate Tiny, and our friend Jagger."

Tiny and Jagger say what's up to everyone, and then they step back to let Sloan do her social butterfly thing. Sloan is a bit of an attention hog, and so we kind of just let her go and do her thing when we're all out. It's much easier that way.

Jagger leans back on the banister with a grin, his eyes trained on me. If I didn't know better, I would say that he is looking at me with interest, but that would probably just be wishful thinking on my part. He mouths the words for me to come over and talk to him. My first reaction is to smile and get up, but I feel kind of slutty about it when I do, because Roman is watching me like a hawk with a scowl on his face, and well, you know, he did just have his face between my legs not that long ago.

"Hey, Elizabeth. How are you? Long time no see."

We're both facing each other, casually leaning on the railing, and I can still feel Roman's heated glare. It's difficult to concentrate with him staring like that, but this is Jagger Reed we're talking about. I need to get it together.

"I recently moved out of my place. So I live with family over in the Historic District."

"Sweet."

"You getting ready for the Olympic trials?"

"Yep, they're next June."

"Oh ... so you have plenty of time."

"Yeah, I'll be training all winter at the club and then probably head over to Nebraska in the spring to continue training."

"Nebraska?"

"That's where the trials are this year."

I can tell that Jagger is a little surprised that I don't know diddly squat about the Olympic trials, but when I was with Ethan that was kind of the point. He didn't want to talk about swimming with me. He talked about it enough with his coach, his parents, and his friends. He would often tell me that I was his very much needed distraction from all of that pressure. I've learned the hard way that his words weren't even remotely truthful. Drugs proved to be the real escape he was searching for. I can't believe how clueless I was. It still stings.

"I'm sure you'll do well and get a spot on the team, Jagger."

Especially because Ethan is no longer competition for him, but I'd never say that. The two of them were always battling each other for the number one and number two spots in competitions.

"Thanks. So how's your–"

"Excuse me," Roman walks up directly between us and interrupts.

"Yes?" I say with annoyance in my voice. He's been a jerk since we left the house, and I'm certainly not trying to talk to him now.

"I brought you your shot."

"Thanks, but I thought I said I didn't want one."

"It's lemon flavored. You'll like it."

He stands close to me, holding the shot. "Take it."

Jagger starts shifting his weight between both of his feet uncomfortably. I can tell he is itching to say something in my defense. That's just the kind of guy Jagger is, but knowing him, I also figure that he is sizing Roman up first. Trying to decide the best way to handle him. Jagger is smart. I've seen him handle some of the drunkest guys on campus quite diplomatically.

"Will you leave if I drink it?" I ask, already knowing that the question is probably going to piss Roman off.

"Why?" he asks icily.

He looks like he wants to rip my head off right now.

"Because the lady and I are going to dance," Jagger interjects with a smile as he grabs my hand. "She's a great dancer."

I'm surprised that Jagger makes a comment about my dancing abilities, because I had no idea that he's ever paid attention to me when we were partying. Although it may not have been the biggest secret in my circle that I love to dance; I'm just shocked that he was watching.

I throw the shot back, grit my teeth from the sour lemon taste, then grab Jagger's arm and we head down the stairs to the dance floor.

Sloan cackles something from her seat on top of Cutter's armrest like, "have fun kiddos," and when I turn around to smile at her, all I see is the deepening scowl on Roman's face.

He's totally pissed, and it brings me a small bit of satisfaction.

NINETEEN

ROMAN

I'M NOT SURE HOW LONG I've been standing by this railing watching Elizabeth and this pretty ass swim boy dance in the middle of my club. I don't like him. I can tell life has been entirely too easy for him. He probably got all A's in school, all the pussy he wants, and lives off daddy's money. He doesn't look like he's ever had to fight for shit a day in his life. Guys like that feel a sense of entitlement about everything. I'm positive that he's nothing but trouble.

Of course one might interpret this another way, and I can't believe I'm even thinking this shit, but is it possible that I'm jealous? I mean, Elizabeth's arms are draped casually across this guy's shoulders, and his hands are holding her tiny waist as they dance way too slowly to a fast ass electro song. They're both smiling and giggling with each other as if they are in the middle of some sort of teen Disney movie or they're out on their first date.

I'm really trying like hell to tame the beast within me, but this is another new emotion for me, and I'm not sure what I can do about it. The swimmer kid should just back the hell off. That would make things a lot simpler, because it would be very embarrassing for everyone if I broke every one of his dainty, slender swimmer fingers, now wouldn't it?

My body is humming.

The hairs across my forearms are vibrating.

This thing brewing inside of my body has rendered me utterly stupid. While it's a sensation that I've felt recently, it's a whole hell of a lot stronger this time.

Possession.

I know it sounds ridiculous, but Elizabeth is mine. I'm not exactly sure how I can feel so covetous of a woman that I have only tasted but not fully claimed. Not to mention that I don't claim women. That's not what I do.

And that's exactly how I know that I'm completely and royally fucked.

I like Elizabeth. I mean, I really like this girl. She's made me laugh more than I have in the last year. She doesn't have fake tits, a fake ass, or even false eyelashes. She's a hundred percent natural, one hundred percent real, and she's super smart. I'm not used to intelligence in the bedroom. I'm used to women who either pretend that they are way smarter than they actually are or are plain ole' home-grown dummies.

I'm actually interested in not just Elizabeth's body (which is perfection, by the way), but in who she is and who she wants to be, which is some brand new shit for me.

Unfortunately though, I am highly interested in a woman who Joseph has made crystal clear is off limits to me. He made sure of that tonight when he called me into the home office.

Hence, my shitty mood all night.

"I have never interfered in your personal life, Roman,

but you're my son, and I know you like the back of my hand. Something's off and if I find out that you are screwing with Elizabeth's head in any kind of way, be assured that I'll cut yours off. She is Juliette's niece. She's a sweet kid. And while she's under my roof, I want you to find out what's going on with her, and then protect every single hair on her head. Including from you."

"I don't know where this is coming from, Joseph, but you're way off base."

I lie through my teeth.

"She had a falling out with her landlord. I took care of it, and I've been watching her like you asked." With my tongue.

"Ask Juliette."

She might have heard me make Elizabeth come like a champion.

I decided not to tell Joseph about Elizabeth's boyfriend and the attack. I think I need to do some more digging, and the old man only needs to know details on a need to know basis. Especially now that he's suspicious.

"Good, because I've made a big decision, and I don't want to regret it."

"What decision?"

"I want to retire from the business and start traveling more with Juliette. I'm going to hand over everything to you. That is if you're ready." I was fucking stunned.

Never in a million years did I believe that Joseph would ever hand his business over to me. I'm not sure that I even wanted it, but I've come to terms that what I want is not the point. I'm already knee deep in this life, and I've done so much crap over the years to build it to this point, that I doubt I'd really know what else to do with myself. This is what I know. This is what I do well. I'm a thug. I'm a monster.

"So how would this work?"

"So you're on board?"

"Yes."

"Okay then, we'll start by me handing The Lotus and the other clubs over to you. I bought them because it will be much easier to control media access to our clients if they use our properties to party in, to get drunk in, to see their mistresses in. Each club will have a strict policy of no cell phone use. So no pictures and no social media posting or check-ins will be permitted. We can block most cell service within the club walls. If they need to use a phone, they'll use the house phone. Celebrities will love it. It's old school. It's exclusive. It's private. You'll eventually have to acquire a few spots in LA and Miami to cast a wide net, but at least we already have New York and Philadelphia on lock."

Using two fingers, my father slid a thick accordion styled folder across his desk with several papers inside, including a ten-page contractual agreement already signed by him and notarized. I picked it up and read it with glazed eyes. I wasn't processing any of the words on the pages.

As crazy as it sounds, all I could think about was how this deal between Joseph and I was effectively eliminating any possibility of me ever exploring this thing with Elizabeth (not that she was necessarily having any of it, but a guy can hope). This was my father's way of saying that I was back in his good graces, that he trusted me, and that there was no room for error. The door to anything happening with her would be ceremonially closed shut if I added my John Hancock to the signature line of the last page.

I signed it anyway.

Yet, as I watch her right now with another man's hands

on her body, I can't help but feel like a man possessed. No matter how sick this shit is. No matter the risk of Joseph finding out. The truth is, is that I'm not even sure I have it in me to stop myself.

She's mine.

"Whatcha doing?" Jade asks curiously while standing behind me.

I didn't even see her walk over. That's how off my game I am.

"Nothing."

"Staring down your cousin's throat while she's dancing with the cutie is definitely something. You either want to kill her or him," she says, apparently amused.

I turn my head slowly to look down at the tiny terror.

"Mind. Your. Fucking. Business."

I stick my hand in my front pocket and dig out a couple of M&Ms.

"You're a sick boy, my friend. I hope you know what you're doing. This is Juliette's niece, right?"

After popping the candy in my mouth, I scrub my face several times with the palm of my hand. Gah! Jade knows me too well. There's no point in trying to hide it.

"I need you to do something," I say to her.

"What?"

"First, shut up. Second, I need you to investigate Elizabeth's ex-boyfriend for me. I'll text you the deets later. Third, right now I need you to go over there and dance with the pretty boy."

"Uh ... he seems to have a partner already, asshat."

Typically, I'd enjoy the back and forth snarky banter between Jade and I, but tonight it's grating my nerves.

Everything is grating on my nerves.

"Just do it, Jade."

"Is that an order?" she asks incredulously.

The lines between friendship and boss/employee have always been blurred but respected between us.

"Obviously."

"Fine, then!" she huffs and stomps away.

I don't like that I have to send Jade on this type of ridiculous mission, but Elizabeth won't look at me. I need her to look up at me. Maybe if she did, she'd stop gyrating her ass around the dance floor and putting on a show for good ole' boy. Maybe if she saw my deadly serious face, she'd stop. So that this very strong desire I have to hurt him will dissipate, because I'm itching to smack that grin off of his face.

I watch as Jade orders a glass of wine and a beer from the bar and then two-steps her way over to Elizabeth and pretty boy with drinks in hand. She hands Elizabeth the glass, and she smiles back in gratitude and then hands the dude the beer. She dances with them while talking their ears off about God knows what, and the next thing I know Jade ends up in between them dancing primarily with the swimmer. His eyes seem to be drawn to Jade's boobs, which are sitting up high and proud in her tight t-shirt.

Good, I've identified a weakness. He likes tits.

Elizabeth whispers something in Jade's ear and walks away. That's when Jade looks up towards my direction and gives me the mission completed nod.

Sloan and her friend Tiny seem to still be completely engrossed in one of Cutter's many stories about the celebrities he's met (he's got a big ass mouth), so I go downstairs and cut Elizabeth off before she can make her way back up to our seating section. She's walking with her head down and doesn't see me at first, but stops when she recognizes my boots.

"I want to talk to you," I say.

"Now?"

"Right now. Walk with me to my office. It's just at the back of the hallway there."

I see the hesitance in her face. She's contemplating what she should do as if this was a life or death decision, but I guess my approach may make it appear as if whatever I have to say is life or death. I've been told that even when I smile, thanks to the scar on my face, I still look like I want to rip somebody's head off.

"It'll take five minutes," I assure her.

She looks back over at the swimmer. His eyeballs still stuck to the front of Jade's shirt.

"Umm ... ok."

Relief settles in my gut that she's agreed. Another unexpected emotion.

"So what's up?"

Elizabeth makes sure to stand at least five feet away from me, as she takes a nervous gulp of wine, waiting for me to speak. I've never noticed before, but her eyelashes are long, black, jut straight down and do an amazing job of highlighting her almond-shaped eyes. She's blinking a little more than usual. I figure it's because I make her a little nervous on top of the fact that the alcohol is hitting her bloodstream. She's had a large lemon drop shot and now a glass of wine, which she's drinking like it's a glass of grape juice.

I take a few steps closer to her as she backs up further into a metal desk. I need to be near her, and if I don't keep a handle on it, I'll be inside her next.

"You look so serious, Masterson." She looks jittery. "What is wrong with you? You've been in a crap mood all night."

I take the glass out of her hand, lean close behind her, and place it down on the desk. That's when I catch a whiff of her hair, which smells like pure sunshine, and my dick gets brick hard. I wrap one of my hands loosely around the base of her warm throat, feeling for her pulse. I can tell that she's holding her breath. It's intoxicating that I have this effect on her. She does the same to me. Heaven must be like this.

"Stop dancing for him," I say to her.

"For who?" she asks on an exhale with a look of feigned confusion across her face.

"You know who."

"Jagger?"

I cringe at the fact that she's even speaking his name out loud in my presence, and I'm amazed at how my body responds to hearing it. I want to kiss her so hard right now, that she'll never think or speak that name again.

"Yes," I hiss. "Him."

"What are you doing, Roman?" she asks hesitantly. I recognize the fear mixed with want in her eyes. I know it well.

"I don't fucking know," I admit.

I continue with my exploration of Elizabeth and pull her even closer as I rub my thumb leisurely across her jugular vein. I can feel the blood pulsing through it. She's staring at me now like a deer caught in the headlights, and it's turning my sick ass on.

After I made her come for me earlier, I was rendered speechless. I love pussy like the next man, but I could write sonnets about the way hers yielded to me. The addictive scent. The incredible taste. The power of her orgasm clenching onto my fingers for dear life. It was all I could do not to plunge my dick inside her next. So not two seconds after she came, I abruptly told her to get ready for the club, and I left the room to get my head together. She probably thinks I'm a psycho. I told her I don't come back for seconds to any woman, yet here I am again.

I fucking want seconds.

I lower my head down to her lips slowly, because I very much want to taste her right now, but I want to allow her a moment to make the decision. I'm always taking from women, dictating how the exchange of power between us will play out, but with Elizabeth I want something else. I want her total and utter submission, but I need her to want me too. If I'm going to slip down the rabbit hole, I need to know that she's falling right along with me.

Her tongue slides between her lips, and I am relieved that her body is finally relaxing. Maybe she does want this. I slide my hand around the side of her neck while I pull her in further and take her mouth. I softly bite her bottom lip, then lick the top, then once I feel and hear an almost indiscernible sound come from the base of her throat, I take that as an invitation to explore further inside of her mouth.

I am very familiar with the push and pull of a woman's body, her mind and her desire, and it's obvious that Elizabeth is torn with whether to give herself over again to whatever this is that's drawing us towards each other. She is totally in her head when it's clear as hell that her body should be leading the charge.

"I can't decide which is my favorite," I say in a voice so foggy and deep, that I don't even recognize it myself.

She pants heavily. "What are you talking about?"

"Which part of your body. Your lips. Your eyes. Your ass. Or maybe these."

I brush my thumbs gently across her nipples and feel as they quickly pebble.

"Masterson–" she pleads.

Shit, I love it when she says my name like that. All breathy and soft, making my dick rigid and straining to burst through the zipper of my jeans. She's wearing a black strapless top, which I pull down underneath her breasts. I feel a sensation straight to my cock when I reveal her amazing tits.

I go back to rubbing her nipples gently back and forth with my thumbs and as I feel her body tensing with desire; I pinch both of her nipples between my thumb and forefingers with just enough firm pressure that she gasps and leans forward towards me.

I know that I could push things further right now, but since I'm crossing all sorts of lines that could put me in deep shit a second time in one day, I've decided that I need to slow this down. I need to make sure that when it does happen between us, if it happens, that she is practically begging for it.

I need her to be sure she wants this as much as I do.

"What do you want right this moment, Duchess?"

"I ... don't–"

"You don't what?"

"I don't know," she exhales.

"Do you want me inside you?"

"Ummm–"

"Do you want me to stop?"

I'm still rubbing and tweaking her nipples. A few moments longer and I think I could have her fall apart for me just by my handling of them. The faces she's making are a mixture of pain and pure pleasure. But like I said, I want her to steer the ship this time.

"Yes."

If I was a two-year-old kid right now, I'd be stomping my

feet in protest. That one word feels like a huge bucket of ice water dumped over the top of my head. I know by her body language that she doesn't mean it, but immediately I stop everything.

I pull her top back up and step back. She was right to stop this anyway. She deserves better than me taking her on top of a hard metal desk in a nightclub office. She deserves better than me period.

Fuck! I'm pissed. I'm not usually the guy who whines, "why me" about life. Hell, I realize that I'm one of the lucky ones. I made it out of my neighborhood, I live in a luxury penthouse apartment, I drive a hundred-thousand-dollar car, I'm good at my job, and I have no problem getting whatever woman I want on any given day of the week. I have no right to be angry or ungrateful about a thing; so the fuck what.

I'm still pissed.

Why does Elizabeth have to be my damn cousin? Why is Joseph watching me like a hawk? Why did I sign that damn contract? Why is she flirting with this swimmer? And why, for the first time in my life, have I found myself in the middle of a situation that I cannot fix my way out of.

"So ... the swimmer. You'll stop dancing for him, right?"

"I'm not dancing for anyone, Masterson. We were dancing together."

"Well, let me put this another way. I don't want to see you two dancing together again."

"Or what? You'll bury him in the backyard until he grows?" she asks sarcastically.

"We were kids. When are you going to let that go?" I smirk.

"You're still the same badass kid you were back then."

"I'm even worse now. Try me."

Please try me.

"I like Jagger."

I think she wants me to pummel him.

"What do you mean, you like him? I brought you out tonight to meet my friends and see what I've done so far with the club not hang out with Captain America. He wasn't invited. Like him on your own time."

She looks at me pensively for a moment.

"What happened earlier tonight and just now can't happen again, Roman. You know that, right?"

I'm beginning to hate it when she calls me by my first name. I'm seeing that when she says it, it isn't a good sign. Masterson is the man she met a few weeks ago in the club. That name rolls off of her tongue like warm butter and makes my dick stand up and beg. That's who she calls out for when my mouth is in between her legs. Roman is the name of her fucking cousin. The boy who buried her in the yard when she was six. The guy who doesn't stand a chance with her.

"I'm not sure I can promise that," I say in complete honesty, but with regret.

"You're insane. We're cousins, Roman. Juliette and Joseph would freak. My parents would freak. Hell, you avoided me for weeks when you found out who I was."

"Just ditch the swimmer or I'll kick his ass, Elizabeth," I bark out in frustration.

Of course I know she's right. Everything she's saying is right, but my dick seems to be in complete disagreement.

"You're a complete ass, Roman!"

Then she picks up her glass, spins on her heels, and slams the door with a great deal of strength behind her.

Not ten fucking minutes later I find Elizabeth giggling and sitting on Jagger's lap, and just a moment before I was about to drop kick the swimmer in his windpipe, I feel two sets of meaty hands pulling me back from the brink of a night spent in police custody.

Camden and Cutter.

Absolute fun snatchers.

TWENTY

ELIZABETH

I'M ON THE PHONE TALKING to Sloan, with my feet propped up on a pillow, eating a bowl of microwave popcorn and sipping on a glass of ice-cold sweet tea that Juliette made. My brain is completely fried, so I've stopped working on my database for the rest of the night and catch up with my bestie instead.

"He's cock blocking and I want to know why hooker?!" Sloan asks with an accusatory tone.

It's been over a week since we all went out to The Lotus, and Roman has been by the house every single day keeping an eye on me (I assume), but acting like a Grade-A asshole in the process.

He's been meeting with Joseph about whatever it is they talk about with the door closed. Eating a scrumptious dinner prepared by Juliette every night. Working out like a maniac in the home gym (I spied on him once or twice). Never once coming by my room to say hello or bothering to ask me if I wanted a little dinner (selfish bastard). Not talking to me at all. All because I'm the one with the level head. The one who stopped things before they went too far.

If I had listened to him and left Jagger alone that night, he would have thought I was cosigning whatever this was going on between us. And I'm not. I can't.

While I usually tell Sloan everything, I have conveniently omitted all details regarding how I've been allowing Roman to feel me up every chance he gets. If she told me something like that about her cousin, I'd probably send her to a shrink. There's just no excuse.

There are millions of single men out there. Why on earth do I have to be so attracted to a man whom I'm related to? Why does he have to be so incredibly sexy? Why does his smart mouth turn me on? Why does he know how to work my body into a frenzy like no one else? Why does he make me feel completely safe when I'm with him? In fact, it's just dawned on me I haven't once thought about my assault since he's been around.

Why do I miss him?

"I don't know what you're talking about," I lie through my teeth.

And the Oscar goes to...

"I have eyes, Bitsy. It's obvious that tall, dark, and badass doesn't want you hooking up with Jagger. He was cock blocking all night. The question is why."

"I don't know. Overprotective cousin I guess. What do you think?" I'm so comical right now. Acting as if I don't have a clue. "You're the expert."

I'm sure she's nodding her head in agreement. "Usually I can call these things, but I'm not sure about your cousin. He's tough to read. Maybe he wants to make sure you stay single, so he can continue to make fun of your life of celibacy and coding. He can't keep up the jokes if you don't remain the nerdy little cousin he buried up to her eyeballs in dirt."

I cringe at her assessment.

"First of all, I wasn't a nerd. I was a six-year-old. And second, it's actually YOU who makes fun of my life of celibacy. Speaking of which, I don't know what the big deal is about me not having sex right now. It's not like I'm a virgin or a nun. I'm just selective."

"Well, you might as well be a virgin. You're almost twenty-four-years-old and you've had sex with two freakin' guys. Not to mention that you got your head cracked open the minute after you finished having half-ass sex with the second one. That shit shouldn't even count."

She's kind of right ... the bitch.

"Plus, I think it changes the narrative if you actually start dating a hot guy. Arguably a guy who is way the hell hotter than Roman. How's he going to make fun of you then? How's he going to play big brother and drag you all over the city like he has been if you're busy with Jagger all the time? It's so obvious that he wants to be the only one getting laid, and of course he also wants to be the center of attention."

Pot meet kettle.

"That's a pretty convoluted theory, Sloan."

I cut my eyes to the phone as if she can see how annoyed I am with this conversation.

"Whatever."

"You think Jagger is hotter than Roman?" I ask out of curiosity, because throughout her long rant, all I heard was that she thought Jagger was hotter than Roman. And any woman with a pulse would realize just how crazy that sounds. Roman is panty dropping gorgeous.

"Of course! Jagger could be a model for Abercrombie and Fitch. What's not to like? Plus, he really likes you, Bitsy.

He always has. This is your chance with him. Jagger fucking Reed."

I swallow a mouthful of popcorn and think about what she is saying. It's true that I've always secretly crushed on Jagger. He's sweet, he's hot, and he is going to be an Olympic athlete for God's sake. What is my problem? He is my perfect distraction from Roman.

"Or is Roman cock blocking because he doesn't want anyone else getting near your hot pocket? I mean, you two did have some sort of connection before you found out that you were related. He was practically stalking you."

"My hot pocket, Sloan? What are you my ninety-year-old grandmother?"

"Forget about my name for your vagina. The actual issue here is, do you think I'm right? Has Roman made a move over into kissing cousin territory with you?"

"Ewww, of course not. It's you who wants to have his babies." I do my best to laugh her off. "Not me."

"Eh, I'm over it. He's related to you. That would be too messy for our friendship."

Messy indeed.

"You want to see Jagger again, right?" she asks quickly. "He asked about you on Wednesday when I saw him at Java."

I should want to, but all I can think about is Roman's face when he saw me sitting on Jagger's lap at The Lotus, and how I'm getting the silent treatment now. I guess it was kind of slutty of me. Maybe I should apologize to him.

"I think Jagger's just being kind, Sloan. I mean let's be honest here. There's no way he has any genuine interest in me. I've seen him dozens of times over the years, and he's barely said hello. He's Ethan's friend. Not mine."

"You were seeing Ethan then. What was he supposed to

do? Ethan was his teammate. He's making up for it now. In fact, I think the text he sent today should tell you just how interested he is."

"It was a group text."

"He didn't want to assume anything, so he included me in on the text. That's all."

"That's up for interpretation."

"The guy texted us that he'd hopefully see you specifically tomorrow at Java. That is man speak for I want to see you tomorrow at Java and you better be there woman! So I'll ask again. Do you want to see Jagger again or not?"

"Well ... yes but–"

"What are you worried about? Not that cousin of yours, I hope."

I'm not worried about him. It's just that he's got a temper, and he's taking this older cousin thing way too seriously. I don't know what the heck my mom told Juliette and Joseph, but I feel like Roman is on babysitting duty."

"You think your mom told them about what happened at the apartment?"

"Well, I kind of tripped up and told him myself."

"You told him about Ethan!"

"I felt like I had to explain why I didn't think Owen was going to give me the security deposit."

"How about my landlord is a dick. The end."

"Ha. Ha. I guess that would have been another way to go, but you know I'm not a good liar. He could tell that I was hiding something."

"Really? Because you've just met the guy and already he can read you?"

"Like I said, and as you well know, I'm not a good liar."

"You're also not a kid, Bitsy. You're a grown ass woman. Take your butt down to Java tomorrow morning and don't let any of them know where you're going. Just because you live with them doesn't mean that they need to know your every move. Worse case scenario is Jagger doesn't show up and you get some work done while you have a latte. Best-case scenario is he throws you in the back seat of his car in the parking lot and has his way with you for an hour."

"You're crazy!"

We both start cracking up as I gobble down a little more popcorn.

"I wish this was a Long Island Iced Tea instead of a sweet tea," I say breezily. "Okay. You're right. Of course you're right. I'll meet him."

"Good!" I can hear her clap her hands together. "In fact, I'll pick you up tomorrow morning. That'll make it easier. Juliette will think you're out with me."

"Okay, cool. I'll be ready by ten. Hold on it's my other line."

A call is coming in on my phone from an area code I don't recognize.

"Hello?"

After a long pause a woman finally speaks, "Is this Elizabeth?"

"Yessss?" Then nothing.

She hangs up.

I click back over to Sloan. "Sorry about that. Just a crank caller."

"That was kind of long for a crank call."

"She asked for me by name then she hung up."

Sloan was silent for a moment. "Are you okay?"

"Sure. It was probably one of Ethan's many hussies unaware that he's in rehab and that we are completely finished with each other."

"I'm sure it was, knowing him. That's why we're on to project Jagger starting tomorrow!"

"So excited."

"You know I love it when I make a good match."

"I don't know how. You've never been good at it."

"Shut it. You talk too much, girly."

And we laugh and giggle with each other like old times for another hour on the phone, although in the back of my mind I can't help but wonder what or who Roman might be doing right now.

ELIZABETH

AS USUAL SLOAN IS RUNNING late, and I didn't get a good night's sleep, so I'm cranky. Someone called my cell at 3:30am and hung up on me. The same crank caller who's been calling me randomly for the last few days, although now I'm wondering if it was the woman who called yesterday. Hell, I thought crank calling ended in the 90s.

Anyway, since I had the inability to go back to sleep after being so rudely woken up, I jumped on the computer and got some work done. Next thing I knew, it was 5am. Now I have dark circles under my eyes I'm desperately trying to cover with concealer, and I'm totally exhausted.

Unfortunately, Sloan's tardiness has left Aunt Juliette just enough time to seek me out and knock on my door. Which sucks because I really had hoped to sneak out of the house without seeing her (she usually sleeps in on Saturday mornings). I really like my aunt, but I'm just not in the mood to hear how I'm working myself to an early grave and how I need to eat a hearty breakfast before I start my day. My aunt's idea of a hearty breakfast is a plate of so much food that it could choke a horse. Now I completely understand why she exercises like a maniac half the time. She has to, or she'd weigh five hundred pounds.

"Oh, you're dressed. Great. How about we go out for an early lunch today? My treat."

See what I mean.

"You look pretty by the way. I love how you wear so much yellow, Elizabeth. It's so common to see girls your age wear nothing but black when wearing bright colors does so much to improve one's disposition."

"Oh thanks, Auntie, but I kind of have plans with Sloan today. She's actually on her way. Can I have a rain check?"

"No worries. Where are you two going this time of morning? You're usually working on that computer of yours. Not that I'm complaining. It's good for you to get out more, sweetie."

"Umm ... we're going to Java."

"What's that?"

"It's a coffeehouse that Sloan and I used to go to all the time near school."

"I have perfectly good coffee downstairs in the kitchen that you can drink for free. Why would you go pay five dollars for coffee? I've never even seen you drink a cup of coffee."

"Well, you know, it's the ambiance of the shop, plus I'm just trying to be better about getting out of the house and hanging with friends."

My aunt curves her lips in amusement. She knows bullshit when she hears it.

"If it works out," she says. "I'd love to meet him someday."

I FEEL A PECULIAR SORT OF energy as soon as we enter Java and I can't shake it. Maybe it's the sleep deprivation. I don't know. But whatever it is—is making me feel on edge and jumpy, and I'm making Sloan bear the brunt of it.

"This coffee is gross." I scrunch my face exaggeratedly from the bitter taste. "Why do we insist on spending good money on this crap?" I realize that I sound like Juliette right now.

Sloan smiles at me while waiting for the barista to finish making some sort of caramel espresso drink with tons of whipped cream on top. It's totally unfair how she can drink all that sugar and never gain a pound.

"Are you that freaking nervous hooker? It's just Jagger."

She pinches my cheek. "Awww, you're so cute." I smack her hand away.

"Honestly. What grown business owner names their coffee shop Java The Hut?" I ask annoyed.

"Calm the hell down, Bitsy. Everybody loves Star Wars, and I think the name works. So do a million other college students in this city."

"They're not even old enough to know who Jabba The Hut from Star Wars was."

"And neither are we, but we know! Everyone's seen Star Wars." Sloan points towards the other side of the room.

"Make sure to grab the club chairs over there by the window. I'll get up when Jagger arrives."

One of the things that drives me a little nuts about Sloan is that she is constantly injecting herself or her strong opinions into every area of my life. She makes it her mission to fix me as if I'm a perpetually broken gadget.

I'm pretty sure this whole "Jagger likes Elizabeth" kick she's on is her way of getting me over Ethan quickly. I don't know what she's so worried about. The moment I realized that he was alive and well and purposely not contacting me was the moment I got over him. I may not be the smartest cookie in the cookie jar when it comes to men, but I'm not that pathetic.

I expected Sloan to drop me off at Java and go about her business, but what was I thinking? She's probably going to spy on me the entire time I'm talking to Jagger. Making this whole meet up a lot more awkward than it already is. Of course Jagger sent a group text. Maybe he is expecting to see both of us and have coffee in a group. Maybe it's better that she is here. I don't want to assume anything.

As per Sloan's instructions, I attempt to swiftly walk across the room (without spilling any coffee) and grab the three leather club chairs in the corner, as good seating in Java is scarce. For whatever reason, beyond my understanding, the coffee is horrible, but Java is popular. Juliette was right. She probably does make better coffee at home.

One redeeming quality about the place though is that it is quaint. It's a small neighborhood coffee house with beautiful bay windows and cozy seating (when you can find one). There are colorful oil and acrylic paintings by students from a neighborhood art school that cover much of the exposed brick walls. I love how the vibrant yellow, blue, and green colors from the paintings pop against the brick red backdrop. And then of course Java also bakes fresh daily. So it always smells like banana and zucchini bread–which I love.

As we sit and kill time talking about one of Sloan's ex-boyfriends and just how much of a Grade A jerk he is, the uneasy feeling is lingering like a weight on the back of my neck. I keep turning over questions in my head in an effort to identify the source. Is there something important I'm forgetting? My keys? My wallet?

Sloan snaps her fingers twice in front of me. "Bitsy, are you listening to me?"

I jump to full attention. "Absolutely. Dillon is going to regret losing you." Blah. Blah. Blah.

"I stopped talking about him a few minutes ago," she says with a slight attitude and turned up lips. "I'm talking about the new territory I'm up for at my job."

"Oh, really?"

"What's wrong with you for real?" I look at my watch.

"He's not even late yet, Bitsy. We're early."

"I'm just in a weird mood, I guess, or maybe I'm more nervous about Jagger than I thought I'd be."

"Its just coffee. You're stressing for no reason. He already likes you."

As we move on chatting about how Sloan is going to ignore Dillon's calls, the recent police shootings on the news, and the latest celebrity gossip– I feel a pair of very familiar eyes staring at me with a fierce intensity. Sloan notices soon after.

"Oh boy," she says after bowing her eyes down.

It's Roman.

As soon as I notice him, he walks over towards us with long, confident strides and a face that I can't read. He looks like he either wants to fight me or fuck me. I take a long gulp of my lukewarm coffee, while I try to figure out what he wants with me and how to stop my stomach from swishing around like a front load washer.

"Ladies."

That's the most he's said to me in an entire week.

"Hey, Roman," Sloan replies unenthusiastically.

I just stare at the lid of my coffee cup.

"How are you, Elizabeth? Missed you this morning."

Sloan gives me a slight kick in the shins, because it is taking me entirely too long to respond to his question.

"I'm good, Masterson."

The corners of his beautiful mouth turn up into the sexiest grin ever.

Sloan clears her throat. "I didn't get to ask you the other night, Roman, but I wanted to ask you something about that first night at The Lotus."

"May I sit? I mean were you expecting anyone else?" he asks in an accusatory tone.

"Well–" I start to say.

"Have a seat." Sloan gestures her hand towards the empty chair.

Roman plops down and leans into the chair with his long muscular legs stretched out in front of him and his arms crossed across his chest. There is something so sexy about how he leans back in the chair that heat swarms throughout my insides and down to my core. I am annoyed with him for being such a baby all week, but I am also still very much attracted to him. No matter how annoying he is, I still desperately want his hands all over me.

"So about the club," she continues. "Do you know what happened that night we met you? Since you're running it now, I thought you'd have the inside scoop."

Roman's mouth tightens for a moment, but then he answers.

"There were a couple girls arguing, and it got heated. Someone pulled out some pepper spray and the ceiling fans basically circulated the shit all around the club."

"People got hurt, right?"

"Yes."

"Interesting," Sloan says. "None of it was on the news.

I swore there was going to be a whole big story on the evening news or at least the next day, but there wasn't."

"Philly is a big town. Perhaps there was a bigger story that night."

"How hurt were the people?"

"A woman died. Another two were in critical condition for about two weeks," Roman says somberly.

I shudder. That's horrible, and we had no clue. How hadn't we heard about this? Why hadn't he told me?

"Oh my God, how wasn't that reported? I wonder if I knew any of them?" Sloan continues jabbering on and on. I kind of want her to be quiet now. She tends to eventually say something inappropriate if you let her rattle on too long. "Were you there partying, Roman? Doesn't seem like your kind of scene."

Yep, now I really want her to shut up.

"What the fuck does that mean?" he asks, sitting there with his muscular arms folded in front of him and staring her dead in the eyes.

"I mean..." Sloan hesitates. She's searching for the correct thing to say and stumbling over her words. I don't blame her. Roman looks both equally menacing and amused.

"I just mean that—"

He gives Sloan a quick dismissive once over. "Look, I get what you're trying to say, but you don't know me. You know nothing about my scene. Don't speak to me as if you do."

"Sorry," she mumbles.

"It's cool." He turns his attention back to me in a very obvious way. It was purposely dismissive to Sloan, but I have to admit that she sort of deserves it, and frankly I'm just happy that the cold war between us is finally thawing. "So, Elizabeth, who are you meeting here?"

My eyes grow wide. Damn Juliette.

"Who said I'm meeting anyone? I'm here with Sloan."

"I'm not stupid little cousin. You'd rather be in bed and have your head inside that laptop than drinking some damn latte on a Saturday morning. Who are you meeting?"

Fuck it. "Jagger."

"Is this a date?" he asks snidely. "The Lotus wasn't enough for the week?"

"It's just coffee, Roman."

"Then I can stay."

"What?"

"You have a problem with your cousin getting to know your friends? He's a good friend of yours right?" I turn to Sloan. "Can you excuse us a minute, Sloan?" "Absolutely," she grins.

After Sloan is out of earshot, I give Roman a piece of my mind.

"Whatever this big brother, kissing cousin thing you're doing is getting tired. I know Jagger better than I know you. Hell, I know the girl who made my coffee just now better than I know you! You don't speak to me all frackin' week, and then you waltz in here asking me questions about who I'm meeting? How dare you."

Roman leans in much closer to me, and I grip the sides of my chair to hold myself steady. Anytime there's close proximity between us, I feel like I'm going to self combust.

"Did you miss me, Duchess?" He asks in the low, gritty

voice that I'm beginning to desperately crave. "Is that why you're so pissed? Because I ain't going to lie, I missed the shit out of you too."

Don't ask him. Don't ask him. "So why the silent treatment all week?" Weakling!

"You told me you couldn't. You asked me to stop this. I'm trying to stop."

"So coming to Java to spy on me. This is you stopping?"

My phone vibrates.

Jagger: I'm around the corner.

I pause to look up at Roman for a moment and then type. It's not a group text this time, so I know I have to respond. He's definitely coming to meet me.

Me: Only been here ten minutes. See you when you get here:)

"Was that him?" Roman asks gruffly.

"Yes." I say while scanning the room for Sloan and keeping a close eye on the door.

"Why are you so nervous?" he asks tightly.

"I'm not. I just don't think it's a good idea if you're here when he arrives."

"And why the fuck is that?"

"You know why."

"Did you know that my apartment is close by?"

"Really?" I thought he actually lived closer to City Hall.

"You want to see it?"

No, Elizabeth.

"When?"

"Now."

"Roman, you know I'm waiting for Jagger."

"Have coffee with him, then meet me at my place in an

hour. I want you to take a look at my desktop. I think I have a virus or something."

"I'm not a computer expert. I hire people for that."

"You know more about that shit than me. Just take a look. If I have to hire someone, then I will."

This is SO not a good idea.

Correction, I know that this is a terrible idea, but I need Roman to leave right now, and saying yes will probably be the only thing that will get him to leave. Plus, I have to admit that I'm curious. I'd love to see his place. It's probably frackin' inspirational. So I start to rationalize.

I'm just going by his apartment.

It's not a date or a booty call.

It's just me helping him out with his computer. I'd do it for anyone else. I'd do it for a stranger. So why not him?

You know why, Elizabeth.

TWENTY-TWO

ROMAN IS JUST A MAN.

Flesh. Bones. Beauty.

That's the mantra I've been repeating to myself in order to mentally prepare for entering his building. For daring to be alone with him in his uber-masculine presence. You would imagine that I could control my internal systems when I am in front of this man, but my circulatory system has a mind of its own.

My blood is racing.

My pulse pounding.

And there's a scary ass Alaskan Malamute named Mr. Tibbs staring me down like I'm a piece of chicken (and not in the good way!), while I am sitting in Roman's living room with my mouth closed, my knees shut, and my eyes completely mesmerized by his inked back. This is not the first time that I have seen him without a shirt on, but to say that Roman's body is a feast for the eyes is an understate-ment. I love looking at him every single time. He's like a Christmas present that has been carefully unwrapped for my viewing pleasure. A treat for the eyes.

Roman is distracted with something when he answers the door in nothing but a pair of snug-fitting, worn jeans that hang low on his waist and a cell phone in his hand. That's probably why he didn't notice how I practically lose my breath, when I look at how his chiseled pecs flex as he motions for me to come in.

But there's something about a man's back, especially this man's back. A broad, strong one with sloped shoulders that looks and probably feels as if it could carry the weight of the world across it. Magnificently adorned with an intricate and patterned tattoo that covers the entire span of it. I've never seen anything like it in my life, and it is on full display as he moves his way around his professionally designed stainless steel kitchen, brewing some sort of latte concoction. Something with chocolate, espresso, milk and a dash of rum or some sort of alcohol. Something which is probably going to taste just as delicious as he looks.

From what I know about Roman so far, I realize that with certain things; he goes about them with a great deal of calculation. He wouldn't be making this drink if he hadn't perfected the recipe. He wouldn't have asked me to come here if he didn't have a very specific reason, and it's certainly not to take a look at his computer.

Like I told myself earlier, this is a terrible idea. I'm not sure why I still came here. I ended up having a good time chatting with Jagger earlier at Java. It was easy. He doesn't intimidate me the way Roman does. He doesn't challenge every frackin' thing I say the way that Roman does. Our conversation wasn't filled with uncomfortable sexual tension or him dragging me to the back and shoving his fingers in my vagina.

We talked about his upcoming swim trials, my app, his little sister, and my cat back home. I only asked him one thing about Ethan, even though I promised Sloan I wouldn't. I just couldn't help it. Although it's obvious that we are definitely done, I'll always be curious about just how deep Ethan was into drugs and exactly what kind of trouble he brought upon my doorstep that night. I also wanted to get an idea of just how completely far my head was buried underneath the sand.

"I don't know much, Elizabeth. I just know that he's been doing drugs and was selling drugs on campus for at least a year. His parents knew about it, at least about the using, but they didn't want to wreck his swimming eligibility by putting him in rehab in the middle of the season."

"Did you know about any of this before the assault at my place, Jagger?"

He sighed. "I'm not going to lie to you. I knew a little about what Ethan was into. Everybody did, but I had no idea he was involved with dealers like that."

When I thought back to certain conversations between Ethan and I, certain nights out, there were definitely red flags. Every time I thought something was off between us, it was probably because he was high, and I just didn't know what being high looked like. I didn't even start really drinking wine until well after I turned twenty-one.

"Do you think they'll come after me again ... those men?"

Jagger picks up one of my hands gently. "No, they weren't after you. You were just in the wrong place at the wrong time. They followed him to your house, but they didn't target you specifically. Plus, they got their pound of flesh already. They wanted to teach Ethan a lesson and they did. It's over. Don't worry," he says sweetly.

A soft ballad plays through a Bluetooth speaker in Roman's living room, which snaps me back to reality.

"I think you'll like this, Duchess."

Roman turns and hands me a cream-colored mug with gold around the rim. It's hot to the touch. I sip it carefully, so I won't burn my tongue. It's absolutely delicious, like I knew it would be. I still don't say much of anything, because there's a heart wrenching song playing through his sound system that I find myself listening attentively to. I'm not familiar with the group, but they are provocatively singing about seduction, passion, and pain.

"How is it?" Roman asks as he sits down carefully next to me with a matching mug of his own. "As good as Java's?"

When he relaxes on the couch next to me, Mr. Tibbs finally relaxes and goes to lie down in what seems to be his special corner of the room. Thank God.

"Better. It's delicious."

He nods with satisfaction, takes a sip from his mug, then carefully places it down on the coffee table. I can't help but stare at his hands when he does. They're big and strong like the rest of Roman, and they're very close to the hem of my flouncy skirt, so I press my knees together even tighter. He's being too polite. Too nice. I don't trust it. I don't trust myself.

"I want to know something, Duchess."

He holds my eyes steady with his own.

I swallow hard.

"What is it?"

"This."

He takes his hand and glides it slowly under my skirt and between my legs while never taking his eyes off of me.

"Open," he commands softly, and I obey.

His fingers gently rub across the seam of the lace trim of my bikini panties several times and then as my eyelids grow heavy, they carefully slide the crotch of my panties to the side.

By this point my eyes are closed for probably several reasons. One being that I can't believe that I'm allowing him to do this ... again. Another being that it feels so good that I wish he'd never stop.

Suddenly his fingers stop moving, and like a switch my lids flick open.

"First, I need you to hand me the mug," he instructs me in a very thick voice. So I place it on the side table as he nods in approval.

"Second, I need you to keep your eyes wide open and on me."

I swallow slowly, as if there's a thick piece of caramel candy sliding down my throat.

"Third—" Then his fingers start methodically moving again up and around but never directly against my clit. "You're soaking wet."

I instinctively clamp my legs shut. He stops moving his fingers again and smiles.

"It's ok. I was just checking, Duchess."

The smug bastard slides the crotch of my panties back in its rightful position and gives the top of my pussy two soft pats before sliding my skirt back in place. If it's even humanly possible, I got even wetter and my throat tighter.

He stands up and holds his hand out to mine. "Let's dance."

What. The. Frack.

I don't even know how I can possibly dance to an emotionally charged song like this after what just happened. He's playing head games with me. I may not be the most experienced player on the block, but I know when I'm outmatched.

"I don't dance." I keep my arms tight to my sides.

"We danced at my father's party."

"That was different."

"You swayed those hips like a pro in The Lotus before everything went down."

It just dawns on me. "Was that you in the corner?" I ask with a whisper. "Watching me that night?"

He smiles and grabs my hand to pull me up.

"This is one of my favorite songs." Is all he says in response. "Come on."

"Well, was it you?"

He exhales slowly in frustration with me. "I told you I spotted you the moment you entered the club, did I not?"

When he grabs my waist and stares down at me, I reluctantly raise my arms and stretch them around his neck. Clasping my hands together. He pulls me in a little further to him and I smell chocolate, coffee and him. So I do the only thing a girl could do in this position who's losing herself to distraction. I rest the side of my face against his naked chest and sway to the hypnotic melody of the song and the singer.

I've never felt so warm, and so wanted. Like I'm exactly in the place where I'm supposed to be.

Actually, I'm in a shitload of trouble.

When the song ends, Roman takes a seat on his sofa and pulls me down next to him. With one arm around my shoulder, he uses the other to pick up the remote and turn the flat screen on.

"Not much on in the middle of a Saturday. Want to order a movie?"

He's fingering some of my hair with his free hand.

"I'm supposed to be taking a look at your desktop, remember?"

"We've got plenty of time for that. Finish your latte."

He leans across me and hands me my mug. The maneuver is obvious. The entire span of his bare torso is in front of my face. If his objective is to tempt me enough to want to lick his chest, he's damn close to mission accomplished.

"Thanks," I say sarcastically.

He chuckles.

"Pick a movie or else we'll do an activity of my choosing."

"I want to talk instead," I say.

"About?"

"I need some dating advice."

Roman unwraps his arm from around my shoulder and lifts my chin up to look directly in his eyes.

"For dating who?"

I nervously clear my throat. "After coffee today, Jagger asked me out on a date. I said yes but then he said he'd call me to firm up an exact date and time."

"You said yes," he repeats in an icy tone. "Elizabeth, I just had my hand inbetween your legs not longer than five minutes ago."

"I like him. He's ... easy."

"And what am I, Elizabeth?"

"You're...my cousin."

"I'm your what?"

Roman starts to slide his hand back underneath my skirt and along the inside of my thigh.

"Your what?" he asks again.

His fingers skillfully slide under the side of my panties and then he rips them apart with a single firm tug.

"Roman, please." I beg prayerfully.

"Your. What." He repeats in a husky voice that's filled with promise of more to come.

He slides one of his fingers inside me, and I inhale harshly from the sudden but welcome intrusion.

I hate how wet I am.

I hate that he knows how my body responds so willingly to his voice and his touch.

There is no hiding between us. I'm unable to feign discomfort at the fact that we're cousins, because my body betrays me every frackin' time. My body is doing all the talking and it's saying, "who gives a shit."

"What's my name, Duchess?"

"Roman, I–"

"Uh-uh. That's not what you call me." I think for a minute. Oh...

"Masterson."

"That's right, baby. My dick gets so hard when you call me Masterson. When you call out my name in a few minutes, that's the name I better hear."

I close my eyes as he gives me that visual. Me calling out his name. And I get even wetter.

"Open those beautiful fucking eyes, Duchess. I want them on me. I want to watch them tear up when I make you fall apart for me again. Eyes. On. Me."

He slides a second finger in. Pumping them rhythmically in and out of my core with the deep precision of a pro. How he talks to me, what he's doing to me, it's all so ridiculously addictive. I want more. I need more.

"Please–"

"Shhh, Duchess. When it's time for you to beg, I'll tell you baby."

Then he stops completely.

I watch him with bated breath as he gets down on the

floor on his knees directly in front of me and stares at me with great intensity before he speaks again. I can feel my heartbeat all the way up in the middle of my throat.

"Ask me what I plan on doing with your body, Duchess."

My breaths are shallow. "What do you mean—"

"I gave you clear direction. Take it. I said to ask me what I plan on doing with your body."

Oh God.

"Whaaa ... what do you plan on doing with my body, Masterson?"

He smiles wickedly.

"I'm going to have you lift up this pretty skirt all the way to your waist, and you're lucky I don't tear this fucking thing to shreds, because I know you wore it specifically for the swimmer. Nevertheless, you're going to lift that skirt up high for me. Then ask me what comes next, Duchess."

Both of his hands are under my skirt now. Kneading my thighs and the crease of where my thighs meet my hips. Thumbs rubbing all around the outside of my labia. It feels a bit like torture and a lot like heaven. When I open my mouth to respond, nothing but soft moans escape.

"Ask me, Duchess." He says again as my massage becomes firmer and deeper, just like the bass in his voice.

"What are you going to do next?" I manage to get out.

"I'm going to spread your legs wide while you stretch your arms across the back of the sofa and you're going to keep them there. Now ask me what's next, Masterson."

"What's next?" I gasp as my head falls back as he starts to softly kiss the inside of my knees. I know it's just a matter of time before he starts working his way up. Roman seems to really enjoy being between my legs, but not more than I like him being there. I'm aching for him. I need to come.

He stops all movement again, and I would yell out of utter aggravation if I didn't think it would inspire him to do something far worse. I think he's taking great pleasure in this game of denying me.

"You forgot the last part of that question, Duchess."

Wait what?! Oh...

"Masterson." I smile.

Of course. He loves it when I call him by his last name.

"You're fucking up, Duchess. Start over from the beginning."

This time he grabs both of my nipples through my shirt and rolls them tightly between his thumbs and pointer fingers. A most delicious distraction that takes the orgasm that was already slowly building and rolling it straight front and center. I'm about to come hard.

That's when his hands and body back completely away from me.

I want to cry and then kick him straight in the gut for stopping.

"I have one rule, Duchess. Your orgasms belong to me. You'll come when I tell you to come."

I take a second to get control of my breathing as the immediate need to come subsides.

"Lets try this shit again. What do I want to hear?"

"What are you going to do next with my body, Masterson?" I ask in the most business-like tone I can muster.

"That's what I wanted to hear. You're learning. Next I'm going to get a good hold of that beautiful ass of yours, lift you high while you hold on tight, and eat what's mine."

At this point, I'm trying my damnedest to hold off the orgasm that is roaring back like a lioness. No, like a damn dragon. I don't know what his kinky ass might do if I come before he says so. Still kneeling on the floor; he moves close to me again and settles in between my legs.

"Lift your pretty yellow skirt up to your waist, baby."

I can't believe that I'm following his orders, that I'm really doing this, but I can't imagine doing anything else at this moment. I want this. I want him.

"Now spread your knees wide and don't close them again, or I'm going to have to spank that pretty ass."

It's taking everything for me not to allow my head to fall back on the couch. The sensations that are bombarding me are overwhelming. Looking at a man dead in his eyes while you're spread completely open is not an easy task or for the faint of heart. I'm exposed in a way that makes me both excited and uncomfortable. Both are emotions that seem to please Roman.

"Give me my pussy now."

I grip the sofa a little harder. Every dirty word and command he gives me is pushing me farther and farther to the edge of an orgasmic abyss. He uses both of his rough hands to scoop me underneath my ass, lifting me higher for easy access, and then he wastes no time getting to work.

Licking me continually from front to back.

"Beautiful," he says reverently against my pussy.

He stops after a few strokes to rest (I think) and uses his thumb to rub my clit back and forth several times. When my hips start to move in tandem with his handling of me, I can feel a smile spread across his lips.

"That's it, baby. Fuck me back."

I can feel the orgasm winding inside me tightly like a coil. I know that it's going to be a powerful one, because Roman obviously likes to tease and draw the orgasms out. He starts then stops tongue fucking me over and over, and it feels like a roller coaster ride, with hills and valleys but all completely exhilarating. A thrill ride.

But I can't hold on any longer.

Tears start to pool as I try to delay the inevitable.

"Please—" I beg.

I clench my fists into the back of the sofa as I'm about to release, and right before I scream bloody murder, Roman stops and smacks my pussy swift and hard with the flat palm of his hand.

Immediately, I explode.

"Fuck!" I scream.

I see fireworks in front of me and bursts of sunlight in my peripheral vision, and my heart is racing a mile a minute. My arms flop to my sides as I'm loose as a noodle and panting heavily. I buck a little as a few aftershocks run through me. Roman allows me a moment to come down, but for no more than a moment. He flips me over so I'm on my knees and leaning over the edge of the sofa. I don't see this one coming, but hear and feel it as he gives me another whack, but this time across the ass.

"Next time you wait until I say you can come, Duchess.

Nod if you understand."

I nod yes. Still breathless. Still blissful.

"Sit back on your heels and raise your arms, baby." I hesitate for a moment.

"I just want to take your shirt off, so I can kiss your back."

It takes every bit of strength I have, but I raise my arms as Roman slowly peels my tank top above my head. Then he unsnaps my bra and lets that fall on the floor behind the sofa. My breasts feel heavier than normal and my nipples as hard as stone as he slides his huge hands around the front of me and tenderly massages them. He continues his massage as he talks to me.

"You smell so fucking good, Duchess. You feel so good," he says while tenderly kissing me in the center of my back. "I just want to bury my dick so far inside you, that you'll never want easy again. You'll always want hard."

At this point, I'm moaning like some wounded animal. I need more relief. I need him inside me. I know this is him forcing my hand. Making me choose between him and Jagger, as if there is really a choice, but I don't want to think about that right now. I don't want to consider the ramifications of my actions. I just want penetration.

"What do you want, Duchess? You want it easy or hard?"

"Hard." I moan telling him what he wants to hear, so that I can get what I need.

"Say again?"

"HARD," I retort angrily.

He chuckles. "Right answer, baby."

I hear Roman's zipper coming down, and then what I think is a foil packet being ripped open. I turn my head and watch as he slides a condom on the biggest cock I've ever seen in my life.

"Wait, Roman–"

He whacks my ass.

"Who's, Roman?" he asks sarcastically.

"I just don't know if I can handle that."

He turns me around to face him while still continuing to massage my breasts, my shoulders, my back. I can't help but lean into him as he talks. It feels so damn good.

"You've had sex before right?"

"Yes." I say emphatically.

"A lot?"

"Not exactly."

"What about with the coke head?"

I roll my eyes. "Once."

I can't read his face right now, but he seems ... pleased.

"I'm going to sit down and you're going to straddle me. Then I'm going to suck those beautiful tits of yours while you slowly take your time sitting down on my dick. You control the tempo and the depth this time. The only rule I have is simple. Don't come until I give you permission,

Duchess. All your orgasms belong to me. All of them."

"That's not easy."

"Nothing good ever is baby."

"Okay," I whisper nervously.

I've never ridden someone, although I know they do it a lot in movies. I'm hoping I can figure it out, or at least fake it. The few times my high school boyfriend Roger and I found time to have sex, it was strictly missionary style and lasted ten minutes tops.

Roman lifts me up with brute strength and sits on the couch while he simultaneously straddles me across his lap. His penis is so hard that it looks brutally angry. Like it's ready to punish me for making it wait so long. I can't imagine how it's going to fit inside of me.

"It's going to be fine, baby. I'm a pro at this."

Somehow that doesn't really make me feel any better. Until he does three things.

First, he closes his warm mouth around one of my nipples. Sucking, then licking, then kissing, and then he does it all over again to the other breast. The sensation of his teeth lightly grazing my nipples makes my hips move with a mind of their own. As my hips gyrate, Roman takes his right hand and very lightly slaps each side of my butt. A tap on the left cheek. Then a tap on the right. Back and forth. And as if all of this wasn't enough, he then takes the thumb of his left hand and lightly rubs my clit.

"Masterson," I say with adoration.

"You're getting nice and wet for me, baby. That's a good girl. I'm not going to stop what I'm doing. You just start lowering yourself down," he says coaxing me. "Go slow."

Things get tricky right from the start as I lower myself on his blunt tip. He is thick and wide and I can feel myself being unnaturally pulled and stretched.

"A little lower, Duchess."

The slaps on my ass grow a little firmer and a little louder. Which immediately sends a gush in between my legs, so I am able to slide down a little further.

"That feels so fucking good. A little further baby." He says with a mouth full of my nipple.

With deep concentration and my eyes tightly shut, I continue to ease my way down and am almost full to the hilt when I feel a hard smack on my butt.

"Eyes on me, Duchess."

He's a genius because that smack was just the little push I needed to come completely down.

Oh. My. God.

I feel full and stretched beyond measure, but it also feels utterly amazing.

He uses both of his hands to knead my ass cheeks, which helps my hips build a rhythmic rocking momentum.

Forward and back.

Forward and back.

After a few minutes, we find a mutual cadence. As I work my hips forward, he pulls me back down, and I feel as if I'm having an out-of-body experience as he strokes me over and over. I'm doing it. I'm riding him. And now I'm also starting to feel that familiar tension build down below. The tension I've only felt when Roman is about to give me one of the most delicious orgasms ever.

This is another first for me. I've never come while having sex, and I think it's about to happen. Now Roman is using his hands to speed things up and bouncing me gently up and down. Up and down. I'm still looking at him. I'm totally concentrating on his face. I'm trying to stay focused and not come.

It's intense and it ain't working.

"You better not be coming, Duchess." He warns with the sexiest grin on his face.

He needs to shut up. The more he talks, the more I'm about to frackin' come. Everything that comes out of his mouth right now is making me crazy. I'm seeing that this is part of his game. He wants me to fail.

"You better ask for permission, Duchess," he says fervently.

I don't know what to say. I barely say anything during sex, much less know how to start asking for shit.

He smacks my ass, and I gasp.

"You know what's coming if you don't ask permission, baby. Last chance."

It's too late.

The jackass was talking too much. Everything he says is a turn on, so I scream loud enough for his neighbors to hear, and the orgasm is so frackin' powerful that I feel a rush of adrenaline straight to my head and it almost knocks me dead on my ass.

Nope, I'm dead.

Death by orgasm.

"I have one rule," he rumbles after catching his own breath.

I know, I know.

"And you broke it."

He quickly lifts me up and lays me across his legs on my stomach. He gives me a throw pillow to rest my head on, since my bottom half is on his lap. I notice that his dick is still rock hard and still sheathed in the condom. I can't believe he didn't come yet. Wow.

"Now for your punishment, Duchess."

"What are you some half ass Dom—"

One of his massive hands comes down like a hammer on my left ass cheek and I yelp.

"Ow!"

He doesn't say sorry or ask me if I'm ok, but just continues smacking on me. On the right cheek, then the left. Right. Left. Each one hurting a bit more than the last. I count seven slaps on each cheek when he finally stops to abruptly slide a finger deep inside of me. I don't think I can tolerate another orgasm. I'm pretty sure I'll pass out. Yet somehow I think that's the point. Part of the punishment.

I'm definitely learning. Roman is kinky and dominant and delicious.

"I knew you'd be wet," he mumbles. "Perfection."

Just when he lulls me into full-blown horniness again, here comes another smack.

Whack!

"Masterson—" I whine in between tears and ecstasy.

No response from him. He just continues with another seven smacks on each cheek, then another round of finger fucking. My bottom is burning, but the fingers inside me seem to level the pain out with an equally pleasurable sensation.

At this point I'm screaming, but I'm not sure for what.

To stop or to keep going?

Finally, when the next slap comes, I come hard.

It's brutal.

It comes in waves this time and it makes my pussy pulse over and over.

I'm spent.

Afterwards, I curl in a fetal position on Roman's lap, curl my arms around his waist, and close my eyelids. I know I shouldn't, but this was the closest thing to euphoria that I've ever experienced, and I want to be close to him. That is, until I feel Mr. Tibbs' cold blue eyes staring up at my warm brown ones. I know it sounds nutty, but there's something about the way he's watching me that makes me start to feel self-conscious. Like he's judging me.

"You okay, Duchess?"

I rustle around.

"Yep, just probably should get going home."

"Home?"

"Yeah."

I can't bear to look him in the eyes.

"It's the middle of the afternoon. Why the hell are you leaving?"

I pick up my bra and tank top, ignoring his question, and politely ask him where the bathroom is.

"Where the FUCK are you going? Don't make me ask you again!" He roars violently.

I don't mean to, but I inadvertently flinch from the loud volume of his protest. When I do, he takes a long look at me from head to toe and stares at me in a way I've never seen before. Like he's just realized what we've done and is scared shitless by it too.

"I'm sorry, Elizabeth. I didn't mean to frighten you. The bathroom is straight back and the last door on the left. When you're ready I'll take you home."

After I shut myself away in Roman's bathroom, I snap

my bra back on and fix my clothes. I take a really long look at myself in the mirror and almost gasp. My makeup is completely smeared, my hair is all over the place, and I look like I've been thoroughly fucked ... by my cousin.

I've hit an all-time low. I cry. All I can do now is try my best to rinse my face with some water, hand soap and toilet tissue and promise myself that this will never happen again.

"I'm ready to go," is all I say once I've gotten myself together and out of the bathroom. I think he notices that I've been crying but he says nothing.

We simply leave his apartment and ride home in the Rover in complete and utter silence.

TWENTY-THREE

ELIZABETH

JUST LIKE A DRUG ADDICT, I wake up the next day regretting my hit of Roman. And just like an addict, I promise myself that I'll get clean. Telling myself that I'll make smarter choices from now on. Unfortunately, like a meth head, my addiction for the bad boy is growing stronger and more powerful with each passing day. I've been plotting and planning all morning how I can acquire just one more hit of Roman and then finally quit him cold turkey. But then divine intervention strikes, and that's when it happens.

The call that changes everything.

A woman named Mrs. Daniella Nelson calls and introduces herself as the executive assistant to a Mr. Henry Lambert. Not the junior level money manager that Sloan knows, but the actual head of the entire investment group. The group that has the power to invest a lot of money into my business.

"Miss Hill, we have an unexpected break in the schedule tomorrow afternoon, and I thought this would be the perfect time for you to pitch Mr. Lambert."

Shut the front door!

"Thanks for thinking of me, Mrs. Nelson. I'd love to pitch Mr. Lambert tomorrow. Just tell me the time and I'll be there. The office on North 16th, right?"

I'm going to need to email Krishna and see if he can make a few quick tweaks to my code.

"No, Miss Hill, Mr. Lambert is away at The Atlantis Hotel in the Bahamas attending a conference. He has a pocket of time in between two panels and asked specifically to meet with you. You'll have to fly to him."

I pause for a moment, because my first thought is of Roman. He'll go ballistic if I just leave the country without, I don't know, talking to him about it. Plus, a little part of me doesn't want to leave to do something so big without getting his opinion. Oh, good grief! I sound ridiculous. Maybe this is just what the two of us need. Space. A minute to get our heads together. To remember that we're cousins, not star-crossed lovers.

"Umm, I'm not sure how I'm going to be able to swing this last minute, Mrs. Nelson." I say with regret. The truth is, is that I don't have enough room on any of my credit cards for a plane ticket around the corner, much less to the Bahamas.

"We'll purchase the ticket and reserve your room, of course, Miss Hill. All you'll need to worry about is a great presentation. If you agree, your flight leaves at 8:30am tomorrow. You'll need to get there early of course because it's an international flight. You have a passport right?"

"I do."

"Excellent! So should I reserve your seat and let Mr. Lambert know that you're on your way?"

This is it, Elizabeth. Your Plan B.

"Yes, thank you."

"Okay, can you email me your details? Send me your

full name, birthdate, passport number and all that jazz, and I'll email you your boarding pass. Make sure to print it out and bring it with you to the gate."

"Absolutely, I'm on it right now."

"And, Miss Hill?"

"Yes?"

"Good luck."

TWENTY-FOUR

ROMAN

"WHAT IN THE HAM sandwich happened in here?"

Jade enters my apartment door cautiously; poking her head inside and looking around corners while randomly kicking things on the floor with the rounded toe of her Converse. I forgot that I gave her a copy of my key if I ever became "unresponsive".

It's a safety precaution we put in place just in case I was ever in trouble, and she needed to access my emergency cash or gun stash. She's never had to use it until today, although had to use is a strong term for her being here. I don't need her help at all, and she knows it. She's just being nosy.

"This place is a real fucking mess, Roman, and so are you."

Tell me something I don't already know, you tiny terror.

"Shut up, Jade."

"We really need to talk about how you speak to your employees, if you're going to take over the business. Your people skills suck."

After the awkward drive home with Elizabeth the other day, I called myself giving her a little distance. I know that I moved entirely too fast with her when she was over my place, and that I probably scared the ever living shit out of her. So I thought it was best that I take yesterday off and make it a "No Duchess Day," because when I'm around her, I can't help but want to get inside her in any way she'll allow me to. Her mind. Her body.

Fortunately, my "No Duchess Day" gave me a chunk of distraction-free time to take a serious look over of the ownership agreements I've signed with Joseph, along with my lawyer, and to set up meetings with management of each club. I have a lot of ideas on how to improve productivity and increase revenue, especially now that Camden and Cutter have agreed to be the managing partners of all the clubs.

Unfortunately, though, I now realize why a "No Duchess Day" was a bad idea, because that woman is capable of anything in twenty-four hours. I run by the house under the pretense of asking Joseph to clarify something in one of the contracts and learn from Juliette that Elizabeth went out of the fucking country to meet some investor, without so much as a single word to me.

After that, my brain and my body went on autopilot. Juliette fixed me something to eat, and I have zero idea of what was on the plate. I just wolfed it down while I thought about a hundred ways to get on a plane to the Bahamas with a non-registered gun. I asked Joseph about clause number twelve in one of the contracts, but I'll be damned if I have any recall of his explanation.

Not that it mattered.

It was all a front to get in the front door and put eyes on

Elizabeth anyway. I just needed to know that she was okay. That she didn't hate me. I wanted to know if she had been thinking about me or about what we did. I'd know if I saw her. Elizabeth is easy to read. Those expressive eyes of hers tell the truth even when she does her best to lie her ass off. Especially to me.

Now she's gone.

When I finally made it home, and I definitely don't remember exactly how I got here, I sat down with my old friend Jack Daniels and drank myself into a coma and then later into a violent rage. That thing, that monster inside me, which I desperately try to keep at bay was rearing its ugly head. That thing telling me I'm not good enough. That I'm trash. That I can't be trusted. I start tossing shit all around the place, destroying my own home; my crowning achievement. Because it doesn't mean shit if I don't mean shit to the one person that is starting to matter to me.

So now I'm sitting on my couch, the same couch that I spread Elizabeth across and fucked her thoroughly on just a day ago, and I'm staring at a blank flat screen. Wondering when the hell did I turn into a complete pussy and what I'm going to do about it, because this shit sucks.

"What are you doing here?" I ask Jade in a very annoyed voice like the prick that I am.

"You didn't return my call or text for over eight hours, homie. You know the protocol. You created it. You could have been in jail or dead in an alley somewhere. What is going on? And don't tell me nothing, because we both know that's a bunch of bullshit. Is this about Joseph?"

"No, Jade."

"Your mom?"

"No," I snap.

Talking about my mother has always been off-limits.

"Then what?"

"Elizabeth is gone."

Jade's eyes grow wide with fear, and I know instantly that she knows something that I don't. Why would she react like that?

"What is it, Jade?" I ask with little patience in my voice. "What."

"Do you know where she went?" she asks nervously.

"To the Bahamas. Why?"

"Oh, shit." Jade rubs the palms of her hands nervously up and down the front of her jeans. "You asked me to look into the ex."

"AND?!"

"Well, the boyfriend Ethan ...he's not in rehab."

My chest constricts. I'm not liking this. I'm really not liking this.

"When did he get out?"

"He didn't. He was never in rehab. At least not in Arizona like Elizabeth thinks."

"So where the fuck is he, Jade?"

"I'm ninety-nine percent sure he's in the Bahamas."

Dying to find out what happens next? The Story Continues In Masterson Unleashed (Book Two).

TAP TO DOWNLOAD BOOK 2 INSTANTLY

or binge the entire series by
CLICKING THIS LINK

Paperback readers can grab the entire series from me over at
https://LisaLangBlakeney.com

Masterson
Books 1-5
THE COMPLETE COLLECTION
LISA LANG
BLAKENEY

NOTE FROM LISA

Thank you for reading Masterson and taking a chance on me if I am a new author to you. I hope you enjoyed Roman & Elizabeth's story so far. I really enjoyed writing about those two; and stay tuned because the drama unfolds further between the two of them in a continuation of their story in—Book Two.

I am someone who has always dreamed of publishing fiction but allowed life to get in the way. Writing this series has been one of the most rewarding and challenging experiences of my life, and I look forward to bringing more stories to you as quickly as I can.

Can you do me a quick favor? Could you please leave a review (a starred review only or a written one) for the book on the retailer where you purchased it? Your review will help other new readers find the book. Leave your reviews here:

Amazon - https://geni.us/m1zon

Apple - https://geni.us/m1apple
Google - https://geni.us/m1google
Kobo - https://geni.us/m1kobo
B&N Nook - https://geni.us/m1nook

Thank you so much,
Lisa

P.S. Make sure to *join my VIP readers list* to be notified of my next release.

3 alpha hot brothers and the women they lay claim to
without apology.
Claimed - Camden & Jade
Indebted - Cutter & Sloan
Broken - Stone & Tiny
Promised - All King Brothers
King Brothers Box Set

The Nighthawk Series

Sexy & sweet sports romances set in the professional world
of football. All standalones.
Saint - Saint & Sabrina
Wolf - Cooper & Ursula
Diesel - Mason & Olivia
Jett - Jett & Adrienne
Rush - Rush & Mia
Freak - Freak & Willow
Brick - coming soon!

ACKNOWLEDGMENTS

SO WHERE DO I START? When I was 17 years old and trying to figure out my future, my mother strongly advised me to NOT major in English, because there was no way that she was going to pay for a college degree that would lead me to being homeless and on the streets (her words not mine English majors:). I ended up majoring in print journalism and spending many, many years of my life writing for newspapers, magazines and websites.

Now that I've married, have children, and my mother is ill with dementia, I see just how fragile life is and how important it is to spend every minute of it hopefully loving what you do. So here I am full circle. Doing what I truly believe I was meant to do. Writing fiction and enjoying every minute of it. And of course there are many people who have helped me get here.

First, I want to thank my amazing husband who has been my best friend since I was 18 years old, and who has supported any and everything that I've ever wanted out of life. Without him in my life, I doubt that I would have ever made it back here. Writing strictly for the love of it and not for profit. I also want to thank my daughters who inspire and influence every decision I make in my life. While they can't read any of my work quite yet (or maybe ever!), they support me in all other ways imaginable. I love each of you EQUALLY. I swear:)

Next I want to thank one of my dearest and closest

friends Kelly Green who has listened to me talk about writing this book endlessly for the last few years and has been nothing but supportive and encouraging. Although she doesn't buy into my obsession with romance (If there's no romantic HEA in a book or a movie, I want no parts of it!), she still gets me, and I love you for that Kelly Boo.

I also want to thank another two of my besties: Donna Kinard, who is my quasi beta reader and Robin Broughton Smith who is my #1 cheerleader. Donna reads all the important parts I need read, and gives me honest feedback that always works and makes me a better author. Robin serves as inspiration that following your heart will always lead you in the right direction. Thank you so much for all your encouragement and support ladies.

When I first finished writing this book, I thought to myself that my acknowledgements page would end right about here. I am a total new fish out of water in the world of romance writing. I am also an introvert. I didn't know any fiction authors or bloggers. Not one. Little did I now that there would be several people very willing to help a newbie along. Support me. Encourage me. And without them I know that I would have felt desperately alone.

Thank you to my editor Marla Esposito. (Shout out to all NYU alumni!) You are much more than an editor to me. Let's face it, without you I would have been writing ellipses ... 'til the cows came home, and Elizabeth would have had very questionable and chunky hands:) Thank you so much for all that you do and in the nurturing way that you do it.

Thank you to Liv Morris a.k.a. Obie-Wan Kenobi, an author with a million other things to do other than help me—I'm so sure:) But she took time out of her day to have an actual conversation with me and talk about my career, my book, my writing and just shoot the sh*t. You are a wealth of knowledge and are hands down responsible for me making smarter decisions about my writing and my marketing. Plus you're one funny NYC gal!

Thanks to author Meredith Wild. The first author to ever actually respond to me on Facebook and give me actual concrete advice that I could apply to my marketing and my writing career. Thanks for all your help, your well wishes, and for being 'real'.

Thanks to author Katie Ashley who has to be one of the nicest authors on the planet. You are another author who was very nice to me (via Facebook) when I first considered writing this book, and you taught me that how you treat people goes a long way in how you're remembered. That's why I read all of your books and try to support everything you do. Not just because your work is great, but because you're a great person. I hope to pay it forward one day.

Thanks to author Jordan Silver a.k.a. Madame Butterfly a.k.a. MamaB. A writing dynamo who didn't know me from a can of paint and has served as true inspiration to what it means to serve your readers . Thank you for your kindness.

Thanks to R.L. Mathewson for writing How To Write, Publish, & All That Good Stuff. One of my favorite books on indie publishing from an author who's actually doing it and doing it well:) I really tried to follow most of your advice. I hope I did you proud!

Thank you to Yolanda Ann of Art Of Romance–the first blogger to take me under her wing and give me fantastic guidance on Facebook. I'd like to also thank bloggers: *I Read Him First, the Goodreads New Adult Book Club, Escape N Books, Reading Is My Bliss* and all the other bloggers and Facebook groups who work tirelessly everyday to promote indie authors and their work.

Thanks to The Hype PR, an amazing group of women

who support and help authors get the word out with grace and ease. I look forward to working with you further in the future ladies!

Finally I want to thank my parents for nurturing my love of reading and writing all my life. It definitely is my passion thanks to you both. And I want to thank my Aunt Ruby who regularly sent me bags of romance novels when I was in high school that fed my desire for a Happily Ever After:)

ABOUT THE AUTHOR

Lisa Lang Blakeney is a USA Today bestselling author of contemporary romance sold in more than 28 countries and translated into several languages. Worried that her fellow PTO moms might disapprove, she wrote and published her steamy debut novel Masterson under a different title and pen name in August of 2015.

Thanks to strong reader support of her alpha male character, Roman Masterson, she was encouraged to continue with the series and published the entire Masterson Trilogy the following year. She hasn't looked back since and continues to write novels featuring strong alpha men and the smart women they seek to claim.

A romance junkie for sure, you can find Lisa watching a romantic comedy, reading a romance novel, or writing one of her own most days of the week. If she's not doing that, she's outside in the garden tending to her roses.

Lisa is the wife of one alpha (whom she met in college), mother to four girls, and two labradoodles. Get news on releases, sales and giveaways when you become one of Lisa's VIP readers at : http://LisaLangBlakeney.com/VIP

facebook.com/authorlisalangblakeney

twitter.com/LisaLangWrites

instagram.com/LisaLangBlakeney

amazon.com/author/lisalangblakeney

bookbub.com/authors/lisa-lang-blakeney

goodreads.com/Lisa_Lang_Blakeney

pinterest.com/lisalangwrites